HAVE YOU GOT THEM ALL?

- ☑ 1 The Secret Seven
- ☑ 2 Secret Seven Adventure
- ☑ 3 Well Done, Secret Seven
- ☑ 4 Secret Seven On The Trail
- ☑ 5 Go Ahead, Secret Seven
- ☑ 6 Good Work, Secret Seven
- ☑ 7 Secret Seven Win Through
- ☑ 8 Three Cheers, Secret Seven
- ☑ 9 Secret Seven Mystery
- ☑ 10 Puzzle For The Secret Seven
- ☑ 11 Secret Seven Fireworks
- ☑ 12 Good Old Secret Seven
- ☐ 13 Shock For The Secret Seven
- ☐ 14 Look Out, Secret Seven
- ☐ 15 Fun For The Secret Seven
- ☐ The Secret Seven Short Story Collection

A Note from Enid Blyton's Daughter

Dear Readers,

I am Gillian, Enid Blyton's elder daughter, and I can remember the Secret Seven books being written. They are very special books because Peter, Janet and the other members of the Secret Seven were all real children.

One day, Enid Blyton met one of her publishers to talk about writing a new book. They discussed whether it should be for younger or older children; and whether it should be a mystery, an adventure or a school story.

The publisher laughed and said to her, 'My four children asked me to tell you about their secret society. They call themselves The Secret Seven because their three friends are members, too. They meet in the old shed at the bottom of the garden and you can't get in if you don't know the password! They've even made badges with "SS" on them. They hoped that you might be able to put them, and Scamper their dog, into one of your stories.'

Enid Blyton went home and wrote to Peter, the publisher's eldest son, and asked him lots of questions about the Secret Seven. She sent him some money to buy the Secret Seven a feast. He wrote back and said that they had all enjoyed jelly and chips!

Meanwhile she wrote a little book about the children called *Secret of the Old Mill*, which became the first story in *The Secret Seven Short Story Collection*. So many children from all over the country wrote to her saying 'Please, please write another Secret Seven Story but next time make it longer.' And so she wrote the first book of the Secret Seven series, called *The Secret Seven*.

The real Secret Seven must be grandparents by now. I wonder what their grandchildren think when they read the Secret Seven books. I hope that they enjoy them all and I hope that you do, too.

With love from Gillian

Gillian (standing) with her sister Imogen and their mother, Enid Blyton

Enid Blyton™

A division of Hachette Children's Books

First published in Great Britain in 1954
by Hodder and Stoughton
This edition published in 2006

For further information on Enid Blyton please contact
www.blyton.com

11

A Catalogue record for this book is available
from the British Library

ISBN-13: 978 0 340 91759 6

Typeset by Hewer Text UK Ltd, Edinburgh
Printed and bound in Great Britain by
Clays Ltd, St Ives plc

The paper and board used in this paperback by Hodder Children's Books are natural recyclable products made from wood grown in sustainable forests. The manufacturing processes conform to the environmental regulations of the country of origin.

Hodder Children's Books
a division of Hachette Children's Books
338 Euston Road, London NW1 3BH
An Hachette UK Company
www.hachette.co.uk

Contents

It is illegal for fireworks to be sold to children. We recommend that fireworks should always be stored and handled by adults.

Always follow the Firework Safety Code:

1. **Never** play with fireworks. They are explosives and can hurt you.
2. **Only** adults should light or hold fireworks.
3. **When** you are watching fireworks, stand well back.
4. **Never** go near a firework that has been lit. Even if it hasn't gone off, it could still explode.
5. **Fireworks** will frighten your pets, so keep them indoors.
6. If you are given a sparkler:

Always wear gloves.
Hold it at arm's length.
When your sparkler goes out, DON'T TOUCH IT. It could still burn you so put it hot end down in a bucket of water.
Never give sparklers to a child under five.
Remember you have to be **18** *years old before you are allowed to buy fireworks in the shops.*

[1]

Secret Seven meeting

'When are the Secret Seven going to have their next meeting?' said Susie to her brother Jack.

'That's nothing to do with *you*!' said Jack. 'You don't belong to it, and what's more, you never will!'

'Goodness! *I* don't want to belong to it!' said Susie, putting on a very surprised voice. 'If I want to belong to a secret society I can always get one of my own. I did once before, and it was a better one than yours.'

'Don't be silly,' said Jack. 'Our Secret Seven is the best in the world. Why, just think of the things we've done and the adventures we've had! I bet we'll have another one soon.'

'I bet you won't,' said Susie, annoyingly. 'You've been meeting in that shed at the bottom of Peter and Janet's garden for weeks now, and there isn't even the *smell* of a mystery!'

'Well, mysteries don't grow on trees, nor do adventures,' said Jack. 'They just happen all in a minute. Anyway, I'm not going to talk about the Secret Seven any more, and you needn't think you'll get anything out of me, because you won't, Susie. And please go out of my room and let me get on with this book.'

'I know your latest password,' said Susie, half-way through the door.

'You do *not*!' said Jack, quite fiercely. 'I haven't mentioned it, and I haven't even written it down so that I won't forget it. You're a story-teller, Susie.'

'I'm not! I'm just telling you so as to warn you to choose a *new* password!' said Susie, and slid out of the door.

Jack stared after her. What an *annoying* sister she was! *Did* she know the password? No, she *couldn't* know it, possibly!

It was true what Susie had said. The Secret Seven had been meeting for weeks, and absolutely nothing had turned up. Certainly the Seven had plenty of fun together, but after having so many exciting adventures it was a bit dull just to go on playing games and talking.

Jack looked in his notebook. When was the next meeting? Tomorrow night, in Peter's shed. Well, that would be quite exciting, because all the members had been told to bring any old clothes they could find. They were going to make the Guy for their bonfire at the next meeting. It would be fun seeing what everyone had brought.

Bonfire Night was next week. Jack got up and rummaged in one of his drawers. Ah, there was his money which he kept in an old tin. Jack counted it carefully. There was just enough to buy a firework called a Humdinger. Jack was sure none of the other members of the Secret Seven would have one of those.

'Fizzzzz – whoooosh—'

'Jack! What in the world are you doing? Are you ill?' called an anxious voice, and his mother's head came round the door.

'No, Mother, I'm all right,' said Jack. 'I was thinking of a Humdinger on Bonfire Night and the noise it will make.'

'Humdinger? Whatever's that?' asked his mother.

'It's a big firework that makes lots of bangs and whooshes. I've saved up enough money to get one. Please will you ask Daddy to buy me one when he goes to do the shopping for Bonfire Night?'

'Give your father the money and he'll get you one,' said his mother. 'Oh, Jack, how untidy your bedroom is. Do tidy it up!'

'I was *just* tidying it,' said Jack to his mother. 'Hey, could you let me have some of those chocolate biscuits out of the tin? We're having a Secret Seven meeting tomorrow night.'

'Very well. Take seven,' said his mother.

'Eight, you mean,' called Jack, as she went out of the room. '*Mother*! Eight, I want. You've forgotten Scamper.'

'Goodness! Well, if you *must* waste good chocolate biscuits on a dog, take eight,' called his mother.

Good, thought Jack. We've all got to take something nice to eat tomorrow night, for the meeting. Choc biscuits will be great! Now, what was the password? Guy Fawkes, wasn't it? Or was that last time's? No, that's the one. Guy Fawkes – and a jolly good password, seeing that Bonfire Night is soon coming! Why does Susie say she knows it? She doesn't!

The meeting was for half-past five, in Peter's shed, and all the Secret Seven meant to be there. Just before the half-hour five children began to file in at Peter's gate and make their way down the garden to the shed where the meetings were held.

The shed door was shut, but a light shone from inside. On the door were the letters

S.S., put there by Peter. It was dark, and one by one torches shone on the door as the members arrived.

Rat-tat!

'Password, please!' That was Peter's voice inside.

'Guy Fawkes!' answered the members one by one.

Pamela was first. Then came Jack, hurrying in case he was late. Then George, carrying a bag of rosy apples as his share of the food. Then Barbara, wondering if the password was Guy Fawkes or Bonfire Night. Oh dear!

Rat-tat! She knocked at the door.

'Password!'

'Er – Bonfire Night,' said Barbara.

The door remained shut, and there was a dead silence inside. Barbara gave a little giggle.

'All right. I know it! Guy Fawkes!'

The door opened and she went in. Everyone was there except Colin.

'He's late,' said Peter. 'Bother him! Look, what a spread we've got tonight!'

The shed was warm and cosy inside. It was lit by two candles, and there was a small oil-stove at the back. On a table made of a box was spread the food the members had brought.

'Apples. Ginger buns. Doughnuts. Peppermint rock, and what's in this bag? Oh yes, hazelnuts from your garden, Pam. *And* you've remembered to bring nutcrackers too. Good. And I've brought orangeade. What a feast!' said Peter.

'I wish Colin would hurry up,' said Janet. 'Oh, here he is!'

There was the sound of running feet and somebody banged at the door. Rat-tat!

'Password!' yelled everyone.

'Guy Fawkes!' answered a voice, and Peter opened the door.

Well, would you believe it! It was *Susie* outside, grinning all over her cheeky face. *Susie*!

[2]

That awful Susie!

'Susie!' cried Jack, springing up in a rage. 'How dare you! You – you – you . . .'

He caught hold of his sister and held her tight. She laughed at him.

'It's all right; I just wanted to give your high-and-mighty members a shock. Aha! I know your password, see?'

'How did you know it?' demanded Peter. 'Let her go, Jack. We'll turn her out in a minute. How did you know the password, Susie?'

'I got it from Jack, of course,' said Susie, most surprisingly.

Everyone stared at poor Jack, who went as red as a beetroot. He glared at Susie.

'You're a wicked story-teller! I never told you the password and I didn't even write it down, in case you found it. How *did* you know it? Were you listening in the bushes round the shed? Did you hear us say the password as we came in?'

'No. If I had, Scamper would have barked,' said Susie, which was quite true. 'I tell you, Jack, I heard you say it yourself. You were talking in your sleep last night and you kept yelling out "Guy Fawkes! Let me in! Guy Fawkes!" So I guessed you were trying to get into the meeting in your sleep and were yelling out the password.'

Jack groaned. 'I do talk in my sleep, but who would have thought I'd yell out the password? I'll keep my bedroom door shut in future. I'm sorry, Peter. What are we going to do with Susie? She ought to be punished for bursting in on our secret meeting like this!'

'Well, we've nothing important to discuss, so we'll make Susie sit in that corner over there, and we'll have our feast, and not offer her a single thing,' said Peter, firmly.

'I'm tired of Susie, always trying to upset our Society. Pam and Barbara, sit her down over there.'

Everyone was so very cross with Susie that she began to feel upset. 'It was only a joke,' she said. 'Anyway, your meetings are silly. You go on and on having them and nothing happens at all. Let me go.'

'Well, promise on your honour you'll never try to trick us again or upset our meetings?' said Peter, sternly.

'No. I won't promise,' said Susie. 'And I shan't sit still in this corner, and I shan't keep quiet. You're to let me go.'

'Certainly not,' began Peter. 'You forced yourself in, and you can jolly well stop and see us eating all—'

He stopped very suddenly as he heard the sound of panting breath, and running feet coming down the garden path.

'It's Colin!' said Janet.

There was a loud rat-tat at the door, and

the password. 'Guy Fawkes! Quick, open the door.'

The door was opened and Colin came in, blinking at the sudden light, after the darkness outside.

'Hey, I've had an adventure! It might be something for the Secret Seven. Listen!'

'Wait! Turn Susie out first!' said Peter.

Colin stared in surprise at seeing Susie there. She gave a sudden giggle, and Jack scowled at her.

'What's she doing here, anyway?' asked Colin, most astonished, as he watched Susie being hustled out of the shed.

The door was slammed and locked. Scamper, the golden spaniel who belonged to Peter and Janet, barked loudly. He hadn't at all approved of Susie being in his shed. He knew she wasn't a member!

'Tell you about Susie later,' said Peter. 'Now, Colin, what's all this about? Why are you late, and what's happened? And for goodness' sake, let's all talk quietly, because Susie is sure to be listening at the door!'

'I'll jolly well see that she isn't,' said Jack, getting up, but Peter pulled him back.

'Sit down! Don't you know it's just what Susie would like, to be chased all over the garden in the dark, spoiling our feast and our meeting and everything! Let her listen at the door if she wants to. She won't hear a word if we whisper. Be quiet, Scamper! I can't hear myself speak with you barking at the top of your voice. Can't *you* whisper too?'

Scamper couldn't. He stopped barking and lay down with his back to Peter, looking rather hurt. But he soon turned himself round again when Colin began his tale.

'I was coming along to the meeting, shining my torch as I came, and when I got to the corner of Beeches Lane, I heard somebody in the clump of bushes there. You know there's quite a little thicket at that corner. There was a lot of whispering going on, and then suddenly I heard a yell and a groan . . .'

'Gosh!' said Janet, startled.

'And somebody fell heavily. I shone my torch at the bushes, but someone knocked it out of my hand,' went on Colin. 'Then I heard the sound of running feet. I went to pick up my torch, which was still shining brightly on the ground, but by the time I shone it into the bushes again, nobody was there!'

'You were really brave to pick it up and look into the bushes,' said Peter. 'What was going on, do you think?'

'I can't imagine, except that there was a quarrel of some sort,' said Colin. 'That isn't all, though. Look what I found in the bushes.'

The Secret Seven were now so excited that they had quite forgotten about whispering. They had raised their voices, and not one of them remembered that Susie might be outside. Scamper gave a little warning growl, but nobody paid any attention.

Colin was holding out a worn and battered notebook, with an elastic band round it. 'I've had a quick look inside,' he said, 'and it might be important. A lot of it is in code, I can't read it, and there's a lot of nonsense too. At least it sounds like nonsense, but I expect it's part of a code. Look!'

They all looked. Everyone began to feel excited. Peter turned the pages and came to a list written down one page. 'Look!' he said. 'Here's a list that might be a record of stolen goods. Listen . . . silver candlesticks, three-branches, cigarette box with initials A.G.B., four silver cups, engraved—'

Jack sprang up. 'I know what all that is! My father read the list out at breakfast this morning. It was in the paper. It's a list of the things stolen from the famous cricketer, Bedwall, last night. Whew! Do you suppose we're on to something, Peter?'

[3]

Exciting plans

The Secret Seven were so thrilled that their excitement made Scamper begin to bark again. He just couldn't help it when he heard them all talking at once. He waved his plumy tail and pawed at Peter, who took no notice at all.

'It must be a notebook kept by one of the thieves, a list of things he stole!'

'What else does it say? I wish we could understand all this stuff in secret code. Wait, look, here's a note scribbled right across this page! See what it says?'

'"Gang meet in old workmen's shed, back of Lane's garage,"' read Peter. '"5 p.m. Wednesday." Whew! That's tomorrow. Gosh, we *are* on to something.'

Everyone began to talk excitedly again,

and Scamper thought it was a very good time to sample a chocolate biscuit and perhaps a ginger bun. Before he did so he ran to the door and sniffed.

Yes. Susie was outside. Scamper could smell her. He growled a little, but as no one took any notice, and he was afraid to bark again, he went back to the good things on the little box-table.

'What are we going to do about this? Tell the police?' asked Colin, who felt most important at bringing all this exciting news to the Seven.

'No. I'll tell you what we'll do,' said Peter. 'We'll creep round to that old shed tomorrow night ourselves, and as soon as we see the gang is safely there, one of us can rush round to the police station, while the rest keep guard on the shed.'

It was decided that that would be a good, sensible and exciting thing to do. Pam gave a huge sigh.

'Excitement makes me feel so hungry. Can't we start on the buns and things? Oh, Scamper, you've been helping yourself! Thief-dog!'

'Scamper! Have you really been taking things?' said Peter, shocked. 'Go into the corner.'

'He's only taken a choc biscuit and a ginger bun,' said Jack, counting everything quickly. 'There should be eight of each thing, but there are only seven of the biscuits and the buns. So really he's only eaten what we brought for *him*, the eighth person.'

'Well, he shouldn't begin before we do,' said Peter. 'He ought to know his manners. Corner, Scamper!'

Poor Scamper retired to the corner, licking his lips for stray chocolate crumbs. He looked so woe-begone that everyone felt extremely sorry for him.

The clothes brought by the Secret Seven for the Guy were quite forgotten. The evening's events were much too exciting even to think about the Guy. The Seven made their plans as they ate.

'Gosh, we forgot all about Susie!' said Peter, suddenly. 'We've been yelling out our plans at the tops of our voices. Bother! Scamper, see if Susie is at the door!'

Scamper obediently ran to the door and sniffed. No, Susie was no longer there. He came back and sat down by Peter, putting his lovely golden head on the boy's knee, hoping for a forgiving pat.

'Oh, so she's not there. You'd have growled if she had been, wouldn't you, Scamper?' said Peter, stroking the dog's silky head and fondling his long ears. 'Well, Susie will be most astonished to hear about our adventure when it's over – serve her right for laughing at us and trying to spoil our meeting!'

It was arranged that all the Seven should go quietly to Lane's garage the next night, after tea. Colin knew Larry, a boy who helped at the garage, and it would be quite easy for the Seven to talk to him and admire the cars until it was time to look about for the workmen's shed behind the garage. Then what would happen? A little thrill of excitement ran all the way up Peter's back when he thought of it.

The Secret Seven are on the move again! he thought. What a good thing, after all these dull weeks when nothing happened!

It seemed a long time till the next afternoon. Everyone at the schools the Secret Seven went to was sure that something was up. The Seven wore their badges, and a lot of whispering went on. All the members looked important and serious.

Susie was very annoying. She kept looking at Pam, Janet and Barbara, who were in her class, and giggling. Whenever she passed them she whispered in their ear:

'Guy Fawkes! Guy Fawkes!'

This was very annoying because it was

still the password of the Secret Seven! They had completely forgotten to change it the night before, in the excitement of making plans. Now Susie still knew it. They must change it as quickly as they could.

At four o'clock all the Secret Seven rushed home early to tea, so that they could be off again immediately to the garage. They were to meet Colin there at a quarter to five.

All their mothers were astonished to see how quickly the children gobbled their teas that afternoon, but luckily nobody was made to stop at home afterwards. One by one they made their way to the garage. Scamper was left behind, in case he barked at an awkward moment.

Everyone was at the garage at a quarter to five. Only fifteen minutes more! Now, where was Larry? They must talk to him for a little while, and then creep round to the shed at the back. How exciting!

[4]

A dreadful shock

Colin was already looking for Larry, the boy he knew who helped at the garage. Ah, there he was, washing a car over in the corner. Colin went over to him, and the other six followed.

'Good evening,' said Larry, grinning at the Seven. He had a shock of fair hair and a very dirty face and twinkling eyes. 'Come to help me?'

'I wish we were allowed to,' said Colin. 'I'd love to mess about with cars. Larry, can we have a look at the ones you've got in the garage now?'

'Yes, so long as you don't open the doors,' said the lad, splashing the water very near Colin's feet.

The Seven divided up and went to look at the cars near the doorway and wide windows, so that they could keep an eye on anyone passing. They might see the 'gang', whoever they were.

'Look! Doesn't *he* look as if he might be one of the gang?' whispered Barbara, nudging Jack as a man went by.

Jack glanced at him.

'Idiot!' he said. 'That's my headmaster. Good thing he didn't hear you! Still, he does look a bit grim!'

'It's five to five,' said George in a low voice. 'I think we'd better go round to the shed soon, Peter.'

'Not yet,' said Peter. 'We don't want to be there when the men arrive. Seen anyone likely to belong to the gang?'

'Not really,' said George. 'Everybody looks rather *ordinary*. But then, the gang might look ordinary too. Gosh, I *am* beginning to feel excited!'

A little later, when the garage clock said a minute past five, Peter gave the signal to move. They all said goodbye to Larry, who playfully splashed hose-water round their ankles as they ran out.

'Bother him, my socks are soaked,' said Jack. 'Do we go down this alley-way, Peter?'

'Yes. I'll go first, and if all's clear I'll give a low whistle,' said Peter.

He went down the alley in the darkness, holding his torch, but not putting it on. He came to the yard behind the garage, where the workmen's shed was.

He stopped in delight. There was a light in it! The gang *were* in there, then! My word, if only they could catch the whole lot at once.

Peter gave a low whistle, and the others trooped down the alley to him. They all wore rubber-soled shoes, and made no noise at all. Their hearts beat fast and

Barbara felt out of breath, hers thumped so hard. They all stared at the little shed, with the dim light shining from its one small window.

'They must be there,' whispered Jack. 'Let's creep up and see if we can peep in at the window.'

They crept noiselessly up to the shed. The window was high up and Peter had to put a few bricks on top of one another to stand on, so that he could reach the window.

He stepped down and whispered to the others: 'They're there. I can't see them, but I can hear them. Shall we get the police straight away, do you think?'

'Well, I'd like to be sure it isn't just *workmen* inside,' said Jack. 'They might be having their tea there or something, you know. Workmen do have a lot of meals, and that shed's pretty cosy, I should think.'

'What are we to do, then? We can't knock on the door and say, "Are you workmen or do you belong to the gang?"' said Peter.

A loud bang came suddenly from the shed and made everyone jump. Barbara clutched at George and made him jump again.

'Was that a gun?' she said. 'They're not shooting, are they?'

'*Don't* grab me like that!' said George, in a fierce whisper. 'You nearly made me yell out. How do I know if it's shooting?'

Another loud bang came, and the Seven once more jumped violently, Peter was puzzled. What was happening in that shed? He suddenly saw that there was a keyhole. Perhaps if he bent down and looked through that he would be able to see what was happening inside.

So he bent down and squinted through the keyhole, and sure enough, he got quite a view, though a narrow one, of the inside of the candle-lit shed.

What he saw filled him with such astonishment that he let out a loud exclamation. He couldn't believe his eyes. He simply couldn't!

'What is it, what is it?' cried Pam, quite forgetting to speak in a whisper. 'Are they shooting? Let *me* look!'

She dragged Peter away and put her eye to the keyhole, and she, too, gave a squeal. Then, to the amazement of all the others but Peter, she began to kick and bang at the locked door! She shouted loudly:

'It's *Susie* in there, Susie and some others! I can see her grinning like anything, and they've got big paper bags to pop. That's what made the bangs. It's Susie; it's all a trick; it's SUSIE!'

So it was. Susie, with Jim and Doris and Ronnie, and now they were rolling over the floor, squealing with laughter. Oh, what a *wonderful* trick they had played on the Secret Seven!

[5]

A victory for Susie

The Secret Seven were so angry that they hardly knew what to do. So it was Susie and her friends who had planned all this! While Susie had been boldly giving the password and forcing her way into their meeting the night before, her friends were pretending to scuffle in the bushes to stop Colin and make him think something really serious was going on!

'They took me in properly,' groaned Colin. 'I really thought it was men scuffling there, and I was so pleased to find that notebook when they had run off! It was too dark to spot that they weren't men, of course.'

'No wonder Susie giggled all the time she

was in our shed, and laughed when Colin rushed in to tell us of his adventure!' said Janet. 'Horrid, tiresome girl!'

'She's the worst sister possible,' said Jack, gloomily. 'Fancy putting that list of stolen things in the notebook, of course, *she* had heard my father read them out at breakfast-time too. Bother Susie!'

George kicked at the shed door. From the inside came the sound of shrieks of delighted laughter, and some enormous guffaws from Jim, who, like Doris, was rolling about from side to side, holding his aching sides. Oh, what a joke! Oh, to think they had brought the stuck-up Secret Seven all the way to this shed, just to see *them*!

'You just wait till you unlock the door and come out!' called Jack. 'You just wait! I'll pull your hair till you squeal, Susie. I'm ashamed of you!'

More squeals of laughter, and a loud,

'Ho, ho, ho,' from Jim again. It really was maddening.

'There's seven of us, and only four of you,' cried Colin, warningly. 'And we'll wait here till you come out, see? You hadn't thought of that, had you?'

'Oh yes, we had,' called Susie. 'But you'll let us go free – you see if you don't.'

'We shan't!' said Jack, furiously. 'Unlock the door.'

'Listen, Jack,' said Susie. 'This is going to be a LOVELY tale to tell all the others at school. Won't the Secret Seven be laughed at? Silly old Secret Seven, tricked by a stupid notebook. They think themselves so grand and so clever, but they're sure that four children in a shed are a gang of robbers shooting at one another! And we only had paper bags to pop!'

The four inside popped paper bags again and roared with laughter. The Secret Seven felt gloomier and gloomier.

'You know, Susie will make everyone roar with laughter about this,' said Colin. 'We shan't be able to hold our heads up for ages. Susie's right. We'll have to let them go free, and not set on them when they come out.'

'No!' said Peter and Jack.

'*Yes*,' said Colin. 'We'll *have* to make a bargain with them, and Susie jolly well knows it. We'll have to let them go free in return for their keeping silent about this. It's no good, we've got to. *I* don't want all the silly kids in the first form roaring with laughter and popping paper bags at me whenever I go by. And they will. I know them!'

There was a silence. It dawned on everyone that Colin was right. Susie had got the best of them. They *couldn't* allow anyone to make a laughing-stock of their Secret Seven Society. They were so proud of it; it was the best Secret Society in the world.

Peter sighed. Susie *was* a pest. Somehow they must pay her back for this tiresome, aggravating trick. But for the moment she had won.

'Susie! You win, for the present!' said Peter. 'You can go free, and we won't even pull your hair, if you promise solemnly not to say a single word about this to anyone at school.'

'All right,' called Susie, triumphantly. 'I knew you'd have to make that bargain. What a swizz for you! Silly old Secret Seven! Meeting solemnly week after week with never a thing to do! Well, we're coming out, so mind you keep your word.'

The door was unlocked from inside and the four came out, laughing and grinning. They stalked through the Secret Seven, noses in the air, enjoying their triumph. Jack's fingers itched to grab at Susie's hair, but he kept them in his pockets.

'Goodbye. Thanks for a marvellous

show,' said the irritating Susie. 'Let us know when you want another adventure, and we'll provide one for you. See you later, Jack!'

They went off down the alley-way, still laughing. It was a gloomy few minutes for the Seven, as they stood in the dark yard, hearing the footsteps going down the alley.

'We MUST find something really exciting ourselves now, as soon as possible,' said Colin. 'That will stop Susie and the others jeering at us.'

'If only we could!' said Peter. 'But the more you look for an adventure the farther away it seems. Bother Susie! What a horrible evening we've had!'

But it wasn't quite the end of it. A lamp suddenly shone out nearby and a voice said:

'Now then! What are you doing here? Clear off, you kids, or I'll report you to your parents!'

It was the policeman! Well! To think they

had been turned off by the police as if *they* were a gang of robbers, and they had had such high hopes of fetching this very policeman to capture a gang in that shed! It was all very, very sad.

In deep silence the Seven left the yard and went gloomily up the alley-way. They could hardly say good night to one another. Oh, for a real adventure, one that would make them important again, and fill their days with breathless excitement!

Be patient, Secret Seven. One may be just round the corner. You just never know!

[6]

A sudden adventure

Next day Peter and Janet talked and talked about Susie's clever trick. Why, oh why, had they allowed themselves to be so easily taken in? Scamper listened sympathetically to their gloomy voices, and went first to one, then to the other, wagging his tail.

'He's trying to tell us he's sorry about it!' said Janet, with a little laugh. 'Oh, Scamper, if only we'd taken you with us, you'd have known Susie was in that shed with her silly friends, and somehow you'd have found a way of telling us.'

Scamper gave a little whine, and then lay on his back, his legs working hard, as if he were pedalling a bicycle upside down. He always did this when he wanted to make the two children laugh.

They laughed now, and patted him. Good old Scamper!

Their mother popped her head in at the door. 'Don't forget you're to go to tea with old Mrs Penton this afternoon.'

'My bike's got a puncture,' said Janet. 'It's *such* a long way to walk. Need I go?'

'Well, Daddy is going out in the car this afternoon. He can take you there, and fetch you back afterwards,' she said. 'He'll call for you about six o'clock, so mind you don't keep him waiting.'

The car was waiting outside Janet's school for her that afternoon, with Daddy at the wheel. They picked Peter up at his school gates, and Daddy drove them to Mrs Penton's. She had been their mother's old nanny, and she was very fond of them.

They forgot all about their annoyance with Susie when they saw the magnificent tea that Mrs Penton had got ready.

'Goodness – cream buns! How delicious!'

said Janet. 'And chocolate éclairs. Did Mummy like them when you were her nanny?'

'Oh yes, she ate far too many once, and I was up all night with her,' said Mrs Penton. 'Very naughty she was, that day, just wouldn't do what she was told, and finished up by over-eating. Dear, dear, what a night I had with her!'

It seemed impossible that their mother could ever have been naughty or have eaten too many cream buns and éclairs. Still, it would be a very easy thing to eat at least a dozen of them, Janet thought, looking at the lovely puffy cream oozing out of the big buns, and those éclairs! She felt very kindly towards the little girl who was now grown-up, and her own mother!

They played the big musical box after tea, and looked at Mrs Penton's funny old picture-books. Then the clock suddenly struck six.

'Gosh, Daddy said we were to be ready at

six!' said Peter, jumping up. 'Hurry up, Janet. Thank you very much, Mrs Penton, for such a smashing tea.'

Hoot – hoo—! That was their father already outside waiting for them. Mrs Penton kissed them both.

'Thank you very, very much,' said Janet. 'I *have* enjoyed myself!'

They ran down the path and climbed into the car at the back. It was quite dark, and the car's headlights shed broad beams over the road.

'Good children,' he said. 'I only had to wait half a minute.' He put in the clutch and pressed down the accelerator; the car slid off down the road. 'I've just got to call at the station for some parcels. I'll leave the car in the yard with you in it. I shan't be a minute,' he added.

They came to the station, and Daddy backed the car out of the way at one end of the station yard. He jumped out and disappeared into the lit entrance of the station.

Peter and Janet lay back on the seat, beginning to feel that they *might* have over-eaten! Janet felt sleepy and shut her eyes. Peter began to think about the evening before, and Susie's clever trick.

He suddenly heard hurried footsteps, and thought it must be his father back again. The door was quickly opened and a man got in. Then the opposite door was opened and another man sat down in the seat beside the driver's.

Peter thought his father had brought a friend with him to give him a lift, and he wondered who it was. It was dark in the station yard, and he couldn't see the other man's face at all. Then the headlights went on, and the car moved quickly out of the yard.

Peter got a really terrible shock as soon as the car passed a lamp-post. The man driving the car wasn't his father! It was somebody he didn't know at all, a man with a low-brimmed hat, and rather long hair down to his collar. Peter's father never had long hair. Whoever was this driving the car?

The boy sat quite still. He looked at the other man when they went by a lamp-post again. No, that wasn't his father either! It was a man he had never seen before. His head was bare and the hair was very short, quite different from his companion's.

A little cold feeling crept round Peter's heart. Who were these men? Were they stealing his father's car? What was he to do?

Janet stirred a little. Peter leaned over to her and put his lips right to her ear.

'Janet!' he whispered. 'Are you awake? Listen to me. I think the car is being stolen by two men, and they don't know we're at the back. Slip quietly down to the floor, so that if they happen to turn round they won't see us. Quick now, for goodness' sake!'

[7]

Something to work on

Janet was awake now, very much awake! She took one scared look at the heads of the two men in front, suddenly outlined by a street lamp, and slid quickly down to the floor. She began to tremble.

Peter slipped down beside her. 'Don't be frightened. I'll look after you. So long as the men don't know we're here, we're all right.'

'But where are they taking us?' whispered Janet, glad that the rattling of the car drowned her voice.

'I've no idea. They've gone down the main street, and now they're in a part of the town I don't know,' whispered Peter. 'Hallo, they're stopping. Keep down, Janet, and don't make a sound!'

The driver stopped the car and peered out of the open window. 'You're all right here,' he said to his companion. 'No one's about. Get in touch with Q8061 at once. Tell him Sid's place, five o'clock any evening. I'll be there.'

'Right,' said the other man and opened his door cautiously. Then he shut it again, and ducked his head down.

'What's up? Someone coming?' said the driver.

'No. I think I've dropped something,' said the other man, in a muffled voice. He appeared to be groping over the floor. 'I'm sure I heard something drop.'

'For goodness' sake! Clear out now while the going's good!' said the driver impatiently. 'The police will be on the lookout for this car in a few minutes. I'm going to Sid's, and I don't know anything at all about you, see? Not a thing!'

The other man muttered something and

opened his door again. He slid out into the dark road. The driver got out on his side; both doors were left open, as the men did not want to make the slightest noise that might call attention to them.

Peter sat up cautiously. He could not see or hear anything of the two men. The darkness had swallowed them completely. In this road the lamp-posts were few and far between, and the driver had been careful to stop in the darkest spot he could find. He had switched headlights and sidelights off as soon as he had stopped.

Peter reached over to the front of the car and switched them on. He didn't want anything to run into his father's car and smash it. He wished he could drive, but he couldn't, and anyway, he was much too young to have a licence. What should he do now?

Janet sat up, too, still trembling. 'Where are we?' she said. 'Have those men gone?'

'Yes. It's all right, Janet; I don't think they're coming back,' said Peter. 'Well, I wonder who they were and why they wanted to come here in the car? Talk about an adventure! We were moaning last night because there wasn't even the smell of one, and now here's one, right out of the blue!'

'Well, I don't much like an adventure in the dark,' said Janet. 'What are we going to do?'

'We must get in touch with Daddy,' said Peter. 'He must still be waiting at the station, unless he's gone home! But we haven't been more than a few minutes. I think I'll try to find a telephone box and telephone the station to see if Daddy is still there.'

'I'm not going to wait in the car by myself,' said Janet, at once. 'Oh dear, I wish we had Scamper with us. I should feel much better then.'

'The men wouldn't have taken the car if Scamper had been with us,' said Peter, getting out. 'He would have barked, and they would have run off to someone else's car. Come on, Janet, get out. I'll lock the doors in case there is anyone else who might take a fancy to Daddy's car!'

He locked all the doors, Janet holding his torch for him so that he could see what he was doing. Then they went down the street to see if they could find a telephone box anywhere.

They were lucky. One was at the corner of the very road where they were! Peter slipped inside and dialled the railway station.

'Station here,' said a voice at the other end.

'This is Peter, of Old Mill House,' said Peter. 'Is my father at the station still, by any chance?'

'Yes, he is,' said the voice. 'He's just collecting some parcels. Do you want to speak to him? Right, I'll ask him to come to the phone.'

Half a minute later Peter heard his father's voice. 'Yes? Who is it? *You*, Peter! But – but aren't you still in the car, in the station yard? Where are you?'

Peter explained everything as clearly as he could, and his father listened to his tale in amazement. 'Well! Two car thieves going off with my car and not guessing you and Janet were in it. Where are you?'

'Janet's just asked somebody,' said Peter. 'We're in Jackson Street, not far from the Broadway. Can you get here, Dad, and fetch the car? We'll wait.'

'Yes. I'll get a taxi here in the yard,' said his father. 'Well, of all the things to happen!'

Janet and Peter went back to the car. Now that they knew their father would be along in a few minutes they no longer felt scared. Instead they began to feel rather pleased and important.

'We'll have to call a Secret Seven meeting

about this *at once*,' said Peter. 'The police will be on to it, I expect, and *we'll* work on it too. What will Susie do *now*? Who cares about her silly tricks? Nobody at all!'

[8]

Another meeting

In a short time a taxi drew up beside the car and the children's father jumped out.

'Here we are!' called Janet, as her father paid the taxi-man.

He ran over, and got into the driver's seat. 'Well! Little did I think my car had been driven away while I was in the station,' he said. 'Are you sure you're all right?'

'Oh yes,' said Peter. 'We were half asleep at the back; the men didn't even spot us. They got in and drove straight to this place, then got out. They hardly said a word to one another.'

'Oh. Well, I suppose they weren't really car thieves,' said his father. 'Just a couple of young idiots who wanted to drive somewhere instead of walk. I shan't bother to inform the police. We'd never catch the fellows, and it would be a waste of everyone's time. I've got the car back; that's all that matters.'

The two children felt a little flat to have their extraordinary adventure disposed of in this way.

'But aren't you *really* going to tell the police?' asked Peter, quite disappointed. 'The men may be real crooks.'

'They probably are. But I'm not going to waste *my* time on them,' said his father. 'They'll be caught for something sooner or later! It's a good thing you had the sense to keep quiet in the back of the car!'

Their mother was a good deal more interested in the affair than Daddy, yet even she thought it was just a silly prank on the part of two young men. But it was different when Peter telephoned Jack and told him what happened. Jack was absolutely thrilled.

'Gosh! Really! I wish I'd been with you!' he shouted in excitement, clutching the telephone hard. 'Let's have a meeting about it. Tomorrow afternoon at three o'clock? We've all got a half-term holiday tomorrow, haven't we? We'll tell the others at school there's a meeting on. I'll . . . Sh. Sh!'

'What are you shushing about?' asked Peter. 'Oh, is that awful Susie about? All right, not a word more. See you tomorrow.'

Next afternoon, at three o'clock, all the Secret Seven were down in the shed, Scamper with them too, running from one to another excitedly. He could feel that something important was afoot!

The oil-stove was already lit and the shed was nice and warm. Curtains were drawn across the windows in case anyone should peer in. Nobody had had time to bring things to eat, but fortunately George had had a present of a large bag of humbugs from his grandmother. He handed them round.

'I say, how super,' said Jack. 'Your granny does buy such ENORMOUS humbugs. They last for ages. Now we shall all be comfortable for the rest of the afternoon, with one of these in our cheeks.'

They sat round on boxes or on old rugs, each with their cheeks bulging with a peppermint humbug. Scamper didn't like them, which was lucky. The children made him sit by the door and listen in case anyone came prying – that awful Susie, for instance, or one of her silly friends!

Peter related the whole event, and everyone listened, thrilled.

'And do you mean to say your father isn't going to the police?' said Colin. 'Well, that leaves the field free for us. Come along, Secret Seven, here's something right up our street!'

'It's very exciting,' said Pam. 'But what

exactly are we going to work on? I mean, what is there to find out? I wouldn't even know where to *begin*!'

'Well, I'll tell you what *I* think,' said Peter, carefully moving his humbug to the other cheek. 'I think those men are up to something. I don't know what, but I think we ought to find out something about them.'

'But how can we?' asked Pam. 'I don't like the sound of them, anyway.'

'Well, if you don't want to be in on this, there's nothing to stop you from walking out,' said Peter, getting cross with Pam. 'The door's over there.'

Pam changed her mind in a hurry. 'Oh no, I *want* to be in on this; of course I do. You tell us what to do, Peter.'

'Well we don't *know* very much,' said Peter. 'Excuse me, all of you, but I'm going to take my humbug out for a minute or two, while I talk. There, that's better. No,

Scamper, don't sniff at it; you don't *like* humbugs!'

With his sweet safely on a clean piece of paper beside him, Peter addressed the meeting.

'We haven't really much to go on, as I said,' he began. 'But we have a *few* clues. One is "Sid's place". We ought to try and find where that is and watch it, to see if either of the men go there. Then we could shadow them. We'd have to watch it at five o'clock each day.'

'Go on,' said George.

'Then there's Q8061,' said Peter. 'That might be a telephone number. We could find out about that.'

'That's silly!' said Pam. 'It doesn't look a bit like a telephone number!'

Peter took no notice of Pam. 'One man had a low-brimmed hat and long hair down to his collar,' he said. 'And I *think* there was something wrong with one hand – it looked as if the tip of the middle finger was missing. I only *just* caught sight of it in the light of a lamp-post, but I'm fairly sure.'

'And the other man had very short hair,' said Janet, suddenly. 'I did notice that. Oh, and Peter, do you remember that he said he thought he'd dropped something? Do you think he had? We never looked to see! He didn't find whatever it was.'

'Gosh, yes. I forgot all about that,' said Peter. 'That's most important. We'll all go and look in the car at once. Bring your torches, please, Secret Seven!'

[9]

The Seven get going

Scamper darted out into the garden with the Seven. Jack looked about to see if Susie or any of her friends were in hiding, but as Scamper didn't run barking at any bush, he felt sure that Susie must be somewhere else!

They all went to the garage. Peter hoped that the car would be there. It was! The children opened the doors and looked inside.

'It's no good us looking in the back,' said Peter. 'The men were in front.'

He felt about everywhere, and shone his torch into every corner of the front of the car. The garage was rather dark, although it was only half-past three in the afternoon.

'Nothing!' he said disappointed.

'Let *me* see,' said Janet. 'I once dropped a pencil and couldn't find it, and it was down between the two front seats!'

She slid her fingers in between the two seats and felt about. She gave a cry and pulled something out. It was a spectacle case. She held it up in triumph.

'Look! That's it. He dropped his spectacle case!'

'But he didn't wear glasses,' said Peter.

'He could have reading glasses, couldn't he?' said Janet. 'Like Granny?'

She opened the case. It was empty. She gave another little squeal.

'Look, it's got his name inside! What do you think of *that*? And his telephone number! *Now* we're on to something!'

The Secret Seven crossed round to look. Janet pointed to a little label inside. On it neatly written was a name and number: 'Briggs. Renning 2150.'

'Renning – that's not far away!' said

Peter. 'We can look up the name in the telephone directory and see his address. Gosh, what a find!'

Everyone was thrilled. Jack was just about to shut the door of the car when he suddenly remembered that no one had looked *under* the left-hand front seat, where the man who had dropped something had sat. He took a little stick from a bundle of garden bamboos standing in a nearby corner and poked under the seat with it, and out rolled a button!

'Look!' said Jack, holding it up.

Peter gave it a glance.

'Oh that's off my father's mac,' he said. 'It must have been there for ages.'

He put it into his pocket, and they all went back to the shed, feeling very excited.

'Well, first we find out Mr Briggs' address. Then we all ride over to see him,' said Peter. 'We'll make him admit he dropped it in the car, and then I'll pounce like anything and say, "And what were you doing in my father's car?" I'm sure the police would be interested if we could actually tell them the name and address of the man who went off in Dad's car like that, and probably they would make him give the name of the other man too!'

This long speech made Peter quite out of breath. The others gazed at him in admiration. It all sounded very bold.

'All right. What about now, this very minute, if we can find his address in Renning?' said Jack. 'Nothing like striking while the iron's hot. We could have tea in that little tea-shop in Renning. They have wonderful macaroons. I ate five last time I was there.'

'Then somebody else must have paid the bill,' said Colin. 'Yes, do let's go now. It *would* be fun, but you can do the talking, Peter!'

'Have you all got your bikes?' said Peter.

'Good. Let's just go in and take a look at the telephone directory, and get the address. Mr Briggs, we're coming after you!'

The telephone directory was very helpful. Mr H. E. J. Briggs lived at Little Hill, Raynes Road, Renning. Telephone number 2150. Peter copied it down carefully.

'Got enough money for tea, everyone?' he asked.

Colin had only a few pence, so Peter offered to lend him some. Now they were all ready to set off.

Peter told his mother they were going out to tea, and away they went, riding carefully in single line down the main road, as they had been taught to do.

Renning was about three miles away, and it didn't really take them long to get there.

'Shall we have tea first?' asked George, looking longingly at the tea-shop they were passing.

'No. Work first, pleasure afterwards,'

said Peter, who was always very strict about things like that. They cycled on to Raynes Road.

It was only a little lane, set with pretty little cottages. Little Hill was at one end, a nice little place with a colourful garden.

'Well it doesn't *look* like the home of a crook,' said Jack. 'But you never know. See, there's someone in the garden, Peter. Come on, do your job. Let's see how you handle things of this sort. Make him admit he dropped that spectacle case in your father's car!'

'Right!' said Peter, and went in boldly at the garden gate. 'Er – good afternoon. Are you Mr Briggs?'

[10]

Peter feels hot all over

As soon as Peter saw the man closely, he knew at once that he wasn't either of the men in the car. For one thing, this man had a big round head, and a face to match, and both the other men had had rather narrow heads, as far as he had been able to see.

The man looked a little surprised. 'No,' he said. 'I'm not Mr Briggs. I'm just a friend staying with him. Do you want him? I'll call him?'

Peter began to feel a little uncomfortable. Somehow this pretty garden and trim little cottage didn't seem the kind of place those men would live in!

'Henry! Henry, there's someone asking for you!' called the man.

Peter saw that the other Secret Seven members were watching eagerly. Would 'Henry' prove to be one of the men they were hunting for?

A man came strolling out, someone with trim, short hair and a narrow head. Yes, he *might* be the man who had sat in the left-hand seat of the car, except that he didn't in the least look as if he could possibly take someone else's car!

Still you never know! thought Peter.

The man looked inquiringly at him. 'What do you want?' he said.

'Er – is your name Mr H. E. J. Briggs, sir?' asked Peter, politely.

'It is,' said the man looking amused. 'Why?'

'Er – well, have you by any chance lost a spectacle case?' asked Peter.

All the rest of the Seven outside the garden held their breath. What would he say?

'Yes. I *have* lost one,' said the man surprised. 'Have you found it? Where was it?'

'It was in the front of a car,' answered Peter, watching him closely.

Now if the man was one of the car-thieves, he would surely look embarrassed, or deny it. He would know that it was the case he had dropped the night before and would be afraid of saying 'Yes, I dropped it there.'

'What an extraordinary thing!' said the man. 'Whose car? You sound rather *mysterious*. Losing a spectacle case is quite an ordinary thing to do, you know!'

'It was dropped in my father's car last night,' said Peter, still watching the man.

'Oh no, it wasn't,' said Mr Briggs at once. 'I've lost this case for about a week. It can't be mine. I wasn't in anyone's car last night.'

'It *is* the man we want, I bet it is!' said Pam in a low voice to Janet. 'He's telling fibs!'

'The case has your name in it,' said Peter, 'so we know it's yours. And it *was* in my father's car last night.'

'Who *is* your father?' said the man, sounding puzzled. 'I can't quite follow what you're getting at. And where's the case?'

'My father lives at Old Mill House,' began Peter, 'and he's—'

'Good gracious! He's not Jack, my farmer friend, surely?' said Mr Briggs. 'That explains everything! He very kindly gave me a lift one day last week, and I must have dropped my spectacle case in his car then. I hunted for it everywhere when I got back home. Never thought of the car, of course! Well, well, so you've brought it back?'

'Oh, are you the man my father speaks of as Harry?' said Peter, taken aback. 'Gosh! Well I suppose you *did* drop your case, then, and not last night, as I thought. Here it is. It's got your name and telephone number in it. That's how we knew it was yours.'

He held it out, and the man took it, smiling. 'Thanks,' he said, 'and now perhaps you'll tell me what all the mystery was about, and why you insisted I had dropped it last night, and why you looked at me as if I were somebody Very Suspicious Indeed.'

Peter heard the others giggling, and he went red. He really didn't know *what* to say!

'Well,' he said, 'you see, two men took my father's car last night, and when we looked in it today we found this case, and we thought perhaps it belonged to one of the men.'

Mr Briggs laughed. 'I see, doing a little detective work. Well, it's very disappointing for you, but I don't happen to be a car-thief. Look, here's five pounds for bringing back my case. Buy some chocolate and share it with those interested friends of yours watching over the hedge.'

'Oh no, thank you,' said Peter, backing

away. 'I don't want anything. I'm only too glad to bring your case back. Goodbye!'

He went quickly out of the garden, most relieved to get away from the amused eyes of Mr Briggs. Goodness, what a mistake! He got on his bicycle and rode swiftly away, the other six following.

They all stopped outside the tea-shop.

'Whew!' said Peter, wiping his forehead. 'I DID feel awful when I found out he was a friend of my father's! Dad is always talking about a man called Harry, but I didn't know his surname before.'

'We thought we were so clever, but we weren't this time,' said Colin. 'Bother! The spectacle case was nothing to do with those two men in the car, but perhaps the button is?'

'Perhaps,' said Peter. 'But I'm not tackling anyone wearing macs with buttons that match the one we found, unless I'm jolly certain he's one of those men! I feel hot all over when I think of Mr Briggs. Suppose he goes and tells my father all about this?'

'Never mind,' said Jack, grinning. 'It was great fun watching you. Let's have tea. Look, they've got macaroons today.'

In they went and had a wonderful tea. And now, what next? Think hard, Secret Seven, and make some exciting plans!

[11]

Jobs for every member

The next day another Secret Seven meeting was held, but this time it was at Colin's, in his little summer-house. It wasn't such a good place as Peter's shed, because it had an open doorway with no door, and they were not allowed to have an oil-stove in it.

However, Colin's mother had asked all the Secret Seven to tea, so it was clear they would have to have their next meeting at his house, and the little summer-house was the only place where they could talk in secret.

'We'll bring our old clothes for the Guy and decide what he should wear,' said Peter. 'We haven't even thought about him in the last two meetings and it's Bonfire Night in a few days. We'll need paper and straw for stuffing him too.'

So all the Secret Seven went to Colin's house that evening. They had a fine tea, the kind they all enjoyed most.

'Sardine sandwiches, honey sandwiches, a smashing cherry cake with cherries inside *and* on top, and an iced sponge cake. I say, Colin, your mother's a wonder,' said Peter, approvingly. 'Isn't she going to have it with us? I'd like to thank her.'

'No, she's had to go out to a committee meeting or something,' said Colin. 'All she said was that we've to behave ourselves, and if we go down to the summer-house this cold dark evening, we've GOT to put on our coats.'

'Right,' said Peter. 'Coats it will be. Mothers are always very keen on coats, aren't they? Personally, I think it's quite hot today.'

They finished up absolutely everything

on the tea-table. There wasn't even a piece of the big cherry cake left! Scamper, who had also been asked to tea, had his own dish of dog-biscuits with shrimp paste on each. He was simply delighted, and crunched them up nonstop.

'Now we'll go to the summer-house. We'd better take a candle it's so dark already,' said Colin. 'And don't forget your coats everyone.'

'And the things for the Guy,' said Peter.

So down they all went to the little wooden summer-house, carrying paper, straw, string and safety pins as well as an odd assortment of old clothes. The house had a wooden bench running all round it and felt a bit cold. Nobody minded that. It was such a nice secret place to talk in, down at the bottom of the dark garden.

The candle was stuck in a bottle and lit. There was no shelf to put it on, so Colin stood it in the middle of the floor.

'Have to be careful of Scamper knocking it over!' said Peter. 'Where is he?'

'He's gone into the kitchen to see Daddy,' said Colin. 'He's cooking a stew or something, and Scamper smelt it. He'll be along soon. Now stack your things under the wooden bench for the time being. That's right. We'll look at the clothes when we've finished the meeting.'

'We'll begin it now,' said Peter. 'Owing to our silly mistake about the spectacles case, we're not as far on with this adventure as we ought to be. We must do a little more work on it. First, has anyone any idea where "Sid's place" is?'

There was a silence.

'Never heard of it,' said Jack.

'Well, it must be some place that is used by men like those two in my father's car,' said Peter.

'Perhaps Larry at the garage would know?' said Colin, who had great faith in

Larry. 'He knows a lot of lorry-drivers, and they're the kind who might go to some place called "Sid's" or "Jim's" or "Nick's".'

'Yes. That's a good idea,' said Peter. 'Colin, you and George go and find out from Larry tomorrow. Now, what else can we do? What about the number that one of the men had to get in touch with – what was it now?'

'Q8061,' said Pam, promptly. 'I think of it as the *letter* Q, but it might be spelt K-E-W, you know.'

'Yes, you're right. It might,' said Peter. 'That's really quite an idea, Pam. It might be a number at Kew telephone exchange, Kew 8061. You and Barbara can make it your job to find out.'

'How do we set about it?' said Barbara.

'I really can't explain such easy things to you,' said Peter, impatiently. 'You and Pam can quite well work out what to do yourselves. Now is there anything else we can work on?'

'Only the button we found in the car,' said Jack.

'I told you, it's sure to belong to my father's mac,' said Peter. 'It's just like the buttons on it.'

'But we ought to make *sure*,' argued Jack. 'You know you always say we never ought to leave anything to chance, Peter. There are hundreds of different coat buttons.'

'Well, perhaps you're right,' said Peter. 'Yes, I think you are. Janet, will you see to that point, please, and look at Dad's mac. I know he's got a button missing, so I expect it belongs to his mac, but we *will* make sure.'

'You haven't given *me* anything to do,' said Jack.

'Well, if the button doesn't match the ones on Dad's mac, you can take charge of *that* point,' said Peter, with a sudden giggle, 'and you can march about looking for people wearing a mac with a missing button.'

'Don't be an idiot,' said Jack. 'Still, if it *isn't* your father's button, it *will* be one dropped by one of those men, and one of us ought to take charge of it. So I will, if it's necessary.'

'Right,' said Peter. 'Well, that's the end of the meeting. Now let's think about the Guy.'

[12]

Oh, what a pity!

Colin and Jack took the bundles of clothes for the Guy out from under the wooden bench of the summer-house. The Seven knelt down on the floor to sort everything out. What a lovely job!

'I wish we had a better light than just this flickering candle on the floor,' said Pam. 'It's difficult to see what colour the clothes are.'

Colin pulled out a fearsome-looking mask from the pile of old things. 'Who brought this? It looks like the villain in that play we saw on TV last night.' He put on the mask and hissed menacingly: your money or your life.'

'You look worse than that villain, Colin,'

said Janet. 'I got the mask at a party ages ago and I put it away for Guy Fawkes. I almost forgot where I had put it.'

'It will make a really frightening Guy. I can just imagine him leering down at us from the top of the bonfire,' said Barbara.

'We'd better start making the Guy,' said Peter. 'This is a good big pair of trousers. If we stuff straw and screwed up paper down the legs we can safety pin those old slippers on the bottoms to look like feet.'

'And here's your father's old green jacket, George. We can do the same to the arms and pin my old gloves on for hands,' said Barbara, 'though his hands will look a bit smaller than the rest of him!'

'Look what I've brought,' said Pam. 'I thought it would be much easier to have an old cushion for a body instead of straw and paper. Mother said I could take this old blue one that has been leaking stuffing.'

The Secret Seven began to roll up paper

and stuff straw into the trousers and jacket. It was difficult to see what they were doing with only the light of the candle. As they worked, they heard the sound of a bark, and then scampering feet. Scamper had been let out of the kitchen door and was coming to find his friends. Where were they? Wuff! Wuff!

'Scamper!' called Janet from the summer-house. 'We're here!'

Scamper tore down the garden path, barking madly. Anyone would think he had been away from the seven children for a whole month, not just half an hour!

He rushed straight into the little summer-house and over went the bottle with the lit candle in its neck! Crash!

'You idiot, Scamper,' said Peter and reached to set the bottle upright again. The candle was still alight.

But before he could take hold of it, the

flame of the candle had licked against a bundle of straw. It was alight!

'Fire!' yelled Peter. 'Look out, Pam! Look out, Barbara!'

The straw flared up and the loose paper on the floor began to burn too. The children tried to stamp out the flames but the fire spread faster than they could stamp.

Flames licked at the wooden bench. The old clothes were smouldering, sending out black smoke that made the children cough and splutter.

The seven children hurried out of the little summer-house clutching each other. Scamper, really terrified, had completely disappeared.

They all turned to look back. Fire glowed through the doorway and windows. They could hear a crackling as their things burned.

'We'd better get some water,' said Colin, suddenly. 'The summer-house will catch fire and burn down. Quick!'

They left the fire and ran to get buckets. There was a little pond nearby, and they filled the buckets from it. Splash! Splash! Splash! The water was thrown all over the summer-house, and there was a tremendous sizzling noise. Black smoke poured out of the little house and almost choked the Seven.

'Pooh!' said Jack, and coughed. 'What a horrible smell!'

'It's a good thing your father didn't see this,' panted Peter to Colin, coming up with another pail of water. 'He would be furious about this. There, I think we've about got the fire down now. POOOOOH! That smoke!'

It was a very, very sad ending to the tea and meeting at Colin's. Barbara was in tears. There was nothing left of the Guy but smoke and smell and a nasty-looking black mess.

'It's bad luck,' said Peter, feeling as if he

wouldn't mind howling himself. 'Bother Scamper! It's all his fault. Where is he?'

'Gone home at sixty miles an hour, I should think,' said Janet. 'It's a pity he hasn't got a post-office savings book like we have. I'd make him take some money out and buy another mask for us.'

'We'll have to see if we can collect some more clothes. But I don't suppose people will want to give us any more after this,' said George.

'I hope your parents won't be too cross about the summer-house,' said Jack gloomily. 'At least it didn't burn down, but everything is very black and wet. The wooden bench is a bit charred too. I'll come along tomorrow, when it's dried up a bit, and help you to clear it up.'

They were just about to go off to the front gate when Janet stopped them. 'We meant to choose a new password today,' she said. 'You know that Susie knows our last one,

"Guy Fawkes", and we really *must* have a secret one. Susie has told everyone in our class.'

'Yes. I forgot about that,' said Peter. 'Well, I vote we have "Bonfire". It really does seem a very good password for to-night!'

'All right – Bonfire,' said Colin. 'I'm sorry it's been such a disappointing evening. This is definitely *not* the kind of adventure I like! Goodbye, all of you. See you tomorrow!'

It was a gloomy company of children that made their way home. Bother Scamper, *why* did he have to do a silly thing like that?

[13]

Sid's Place

All the Secret Seven felt exceedingly gloomy next day, which was Sunday. They met at Sunday School, but none of them had much to say. They were all very subdued. Colin's parents had been very cross about the damaged summer-house and had forbidden him ever to use candles there again.

'Scamper *did* race home last night,' said Janet to the girls. 'He was behind the couch, trembling from head to foot. He is awfully frightened of fire you know.'

'Poor Scamper!' said Pam. 'Did you forgive him?'

'We simply had to,' said Janet. 'Anyway, he didn't mean to upset the candle, poor Scamper. We stroked him and patted him and loved him, and when he saw we weren't going to scold him, he crept out and sat as close to our legs as he could, and put his head on my knee.'

'He's so sweet,' said Barbara. 'But all the same it's *dreadful* to have lost our Guy.'

'It's quite put our adventure out of my mind,' said Pam. 'But I suppose we'd better think about it again tomorrow, Barbara. We've got to find out about that telephone number, Kew 8061. Though how we shall do it, I don't know.'

'Leave it till tomorrow,' said Barbara. 'I can't think of anything but our poor Guy today.'

The next day was Monday, and the Seven were back at school. George and Colin went to call at the garage after morning school, to try and find out something about 'Sid's Place' from Larry. He was sitting in a corner with a newspaper, munching his lunch.

'Hallo, Larry,' said Colin. 'I wonder if you can help us. Do you know anywhere called "Sid's Place"?'

'No, I don't,' said Larry. 'Sounds like an eating-house or something. There's a lorry-driver coming in soon. If you'd like to wait, I'll ask him.'

The lorry drove in after three or four minutes, and the man got down, a big heavy fellow who called out cheerfully to Larry. 'Just off to get a bite of dinner. Be back in half an hour for my lorry.'

'Hey, Charlie, do you eat at "Sid's Place"?' called Larry. 'Do you know it?'

' "Sid's Place"? No, I eat at my sister's when I come through here,' said Charlie. 'Wait a minute now. "Sid's" you said. Yes I remember seeing a little café called "Sid's Café". Would that be the place you're meaning?'

'Could be,' said Larry, looking questioningly at Colin.

Colin nodded. 'Probably the one,' he said, feeling suddenly excited. 'Where is it?'

'You know Old Street? Well, it's at the corner of Old Street and James Street, not a first-class place, and not the sort you boys want to go to. So long, Larry. See you in half an hour!'

'Thanks, Larry,' said Colin. 'Come on, George, let's go and have a look at this place. We've just about got time.'

They went to Old Street and walked down to James Street at the end. On the corner, sharing a bit of each street, was a rather dirty-looking eating-house. 'Sid's Café' was painted over the top of the very messy window.

The boys looked inside. Men were sitting at a long counter, eating sandwiches and drinking coffee or tea. There were one or two tables in the shop, too, at which slightly better-dressed men were having a hot meal served to them by a fat and cheerful girl.

'Oh so that's "Sid's Place",' said Colin, staring in. 'I wonder which is Sid?'

'Perhaps Sid is somewhere in the back quarters,' said George. 'There are only girls serving here. Well we know that one of those men comes here every day about five o'clock. One of us must watch, and we'll be bound to see the man.'

'It'll have to be Peter,' said Colin. 'We wouldn't know the man. He would probably recognise him at once.'

'Yes. It's going to be very difficult for him to hang about here, watching everyone,' said George. 'People will wonder what he's up to. Two of us would seem even *more* suspicious.'

'Well that's up to Peter!' said Colin. 'We've done *our* job and found Sid's place. Come on, we'll be awfully late for lunch.'

Peter was very pleased with Colin and George when he heard their news. 'Good work!' he said. 'I'll get along there at five o'clock this afternoon. How have Pam and Barbara got on?'

Janet told him while they had a quick tea together after afternoon school. 'They just couldn't think *how* to do anything about KEW 8061,' said Janet. 'They simply couldn't.'

'Couple of idiots!' said Peter, munching a bun quickly. 'Hurry up, I must go.'

'Well, Pam asked her mother how to find out if there *was* such a number, because she and Barbara really didn't feel they could wade all through the telephone directories,' said Janet. 'And her mother said, "Well, just ring up and see if there's an answer!"'

'Easy,' said Peter. 'Simple!'

'Yes – well, they rang up the number, feeling very excited, because they thought they could ask whoever answered what his name and address were, but there was no reply,' said Janet. 'And the operator said it was because there was no telephone with that number at present! So Q8061 is *not* a telephone number, Peter. It must be something else!'

'Bother!' said Peter, getting up. 'It would have been marvellous if KEW 8061 *had* answered. We'd have been able to get the name and address and everything. That clue isn't much good, I'm afraid. I must be off, Janet. Wouldn't it be wonderful if I spotted one of the men going into Sid's place?'

'It *would*,' said Janet. 'Oh, I DO hope you do, Peter!'

[14]

A wonderful idea

Peter went as quickly as he could to the corner of Old Street and James Street. Yes – there was Sid's Café, just as Colin had said. What was the time?

He glanced at his watch – six minutes to five. Well, if the man came at five o'clock, he ought just to catch him. Of course, he might come any time after that. That would be a nuisance, because then Peter would have to wait about a long time.

Peter lolled against the corner, watching everyone who came by, especially, of course, the men who went in and out of 'Sid's Café'. They were mostly men with barrows of fruit that they left outside, or drivers of vans, or shifty-looking men, unshaved and dirty.

He got a shock when someone came out of the café and spoke roughly to him.

'Now then, what are you doing here, lolling about? Don't you dare take fruit off my barrow! I've caught you boys doing it before, and I'll call the police if you do. Clear off!'

'I wouldn't *dream* of taking your fruit!' said Peter, indignantly, looking at the pile of cheap fruit on the nearby barrow.

'Ho, you wouldn't, would you? Well, then, what are you standing here for, looking about? Boys don't stand at corners for nothing! We've been watching you from inside the shop, me and my mates, and we know you're after something!'

Peter was shocked. How dare this man say things like that to him! Still, perhaps some boys did steal from barrows or from fruit-stalls outside shops.

'Go on, you tell me what you're standing about here for,' said the man again, putting his face close to Peter's.

As the boy couldn't tell him the reason why he was standing at that corner, he said nothing, but turned and went off, his face burning red. Horrible man! he thought. And I haven't seen anyone yet in the least like that man who went off in our car. Of course, all I've got to go on really is his hat and long hair, and possibly maimed finger on his right hand.

He ran back home, thinking hard. After all, that man might go to Sid's place each night and I'd *never* know him if he had a cap instead of a hat, and had cut his hair shorter. And most of these men slouch along with their hands in their pockets, so I wouldn't see his hand either. It's hopeless.

Peter went round to see Colin about it. Jack and George were there, doing their homework together.

'Hallo!' they said, in surprise. 'Aren't you

watching at Sid's place?'

Peter told them what had happened. 'I don't see how I can go and watch there any more,' he said, rather gloomily. 'That man who spoke to me was really nasty. And how can I watch without being seen?'

'Can't be done,' said Colin. 'Give it up! This is something we just can't do. Come on out to the summer-house and see what I've made! We cleared away the mess from the fire, and I've got something else there now!'

They all went out to the summer-house, with their torches. Colin shone his on to something there, and Peter jumped in astonishment, not at first realising what it was.

'Gosh! It's a Guy!' he said, in admiration. 'What a beauty!'

The Guy certainly was very fine. He was stuffed with straw, and wore some of Colin's very old clothes. He had a mask, of course, and grinned happily at the three boys. He had a wig made of black strands of wool and an old hat on top. Colin had sat him in a garden barrow, and he really looked marvellous.

'He's not man-sized because I only had my very old and small suit, but he's the best I could do,' said Colin. 'I bought another mask with my pocket money. Dad said we can have a bonfire at the bottom of the garden as long as he is there. You can all come and help build it tomorrow.'

The Guy seemed to watch them as they talked, grinning away merrily.

'It's a pity *he* can't watch outside Sid's place!' said Jack. 'Nobody would suspect him or bother about *him*. He could watch for that fellow all evening!'

They all laughed. Then Peter stopped suddenly and gazed hard at the Guy. An idea had come to him, a really WONDERFUL idea!

'Hey!' he said, clutching at Colin and making him jump. 'You've given me an idea! What about ME dressing up as a Guy, and wearing a mask with eye-holes – and one of you taking me somewhere near Sid's Café? There are heaps of these Guys about now, and nobody would think our Guy was *real*. I would watch for ages and nobody would guess.'

'Whew!' said the other three together, and stared at Peter in admiration.

Colin thumped him on the back. 'That's a brilliant idea!' he said. 'Super! Smashing! When shall we do it?'

'Tomorrow,' said Peter. 'I can rush here and dress up easily enough, and one of you can wheel me off in the barrow – all of you, if you like! What a game!'

'But my mother doesn't like the idea of children taking Guys and begging for money,' said Colin, remembering. 'She says that begging is wrong.'

'So it is,' said Peter. 'My mother says that too, but if we *did* get any money we could give it to a charity.'

'Oh well, that's all right, then!' said Colin. 'Gosh, this is grand! Mind you don't leap up out of the barrow if you see that fellow going into Sid's place, Peter!'

'I'll keep as still as a real Guy!' said Peter, grinning. 'Well, so long. See you at school tomorrow.'

[15]

The peculiar Guy

Peter raced home to tell Janet of the new idea. She was so thrilled that she couldn't say a word. What an idea! How super! She stared in admiration at her brother. He was truly a fine leader for the Secret Seven!

Scamper wuffed loudly, exactly as if he were saying, 'Great, Peter, splendid idea!'

'*I've* got something to tell you, too,' said Janet, suddenly remembering. 'I looked on Daddy's mac and he *has* got a button missing; but it's a small one on his sleeve, not a large one like we found. And also it's not quite the same colour, Peter.'

'Ah, good! That means it probably *was* a button that dropped from that man's mac!' said Peter, pleased. 'Jack will have to take the button, Janet, and work on that clue, if he can! So give it to me, and I'll hand it to him tomorrow.'

'I wish we could find out about Q8061,' said Janet. 'I'm pretty sure it must be someone's telephone number, but it's very difficult to find out.'

'There's Mother calling,' said Peter. 'I bet it's to tell me to do my homework!'

It was of course, and poor Peter found it very difficult indeed to work out arithmetic problems when his head was full of dressing up as a Guy!

All the Secret Seven were thrilled to hear of Peter's new plan, and next evening they were round at Colin's to see him dress up. He really did look remarkably good!

He wore an old pair of patched trousers, and a ragged jacket. He wore a pair of great big boots thrown out by Colin's father. He had a scarf round his neck, and a big old hat over a wig made of black wool.

'You look quite *dreadful*!' said Janet, with a giggle. 'Put the mask on now.'

Peter put it on, and immediately became a grinning Guy, like all the other Guys that were appearing here and there in the streets of the town. Scamper took one look at Peter's suddenly changed face, and backed away, growling.

'It's all right, Scamper,' said Peter, laughing. 'It's me! Don't be afraid.'

'You look horrible,' said Pam. 'I really feel scared when I look at you, though I know you're really Peter. Nobody, *nobody* could possibly guess you were alive!'

Peter got into the barrow. 'Gosh, it's very hard and uncomfortable,' he said. 'Got any old cushions, Colin?'

Colin produced an old rug and three rather dirty garden cushions. These made the barrow much more comfortable. Peter got in and lolled on the cushions in the limp, floppy way of all Guys. He really looked extremely Guy-like!

The others shrieked with laughter to see him.

'Come on,' said Colin at last. 'We really must go, or we shan't be there till long past five.'

The three boys set off, taking turns at wheeling Peter in the barrow. He kept making horrible groans and moans, and Jack laughed so much that he had to sit down on a bus-stop seat and hold his aching sides.

An old lady there peered at the Guy. 'What a good one!' she said, and fumbled in her purse. 'I'll give you some money for fireworks.'

'Oh, any money we get is going to charity,' explained George quickly.

She gave him fifty pence, and then, as the bus came up, waved to them and got on.

'How nice of her!' said George. 'Fifty whole pence.'

They went on down the street, with Peter thoroughly enjoying himself! He lolled about, watching everything through the eye-slits of his mask, and made silly remarks in a hollow Guy-like voice that made the others laugh helplessly.

At last they came to Sid's Café. The barrow was neatly wedged into a little alcove near the door, from which Peter could see everyone who went in or out.

The boys stood nearby, waiting to see if Peter recognised anyone. If he did, he was to give a sign, and two of the Seven would shadow the man to see where he went, if he happened to come *out* of the café. If he went inside it they were to wait till he came out.

The men going in and out of the eating-house were amused with the Guy. One prodded him hard with his stick, and gave Peter a terrible shock. 'Good Guy you've got there!' said the man and threw five pence on to Peter's tummy.

'Colin! Jack! You're NOT to let people prod me like that,' said Peter, in a fierce whisper. 'It really hurt.'

'Well, how are we to stop them?' said Colin, also in a whisper.

All went well till two young men came by and saw the Guy sitting there. 'Hallo! He's a good Guy!' said one. 'Nice pair of boots he's got. I've a good mind to take them off him!'

And to Peter's horror, he felt the boots on his feet being tugged hard. He gave a yell, and the young men looked extremely startled. They disappeared quickly.

'CAN'T you look after me better?' said Peter to the others. 'Heave me up a bit on the cushions. Those men pulled me off.'

Colin and George heaved him into a more comfortable position.

'Anyway, you've made quite a bit of money,' said George, in Peter's ear. 'People think you're jolly good, we've got quite a few pounds.'

Peter grunted. He was cross with the others. Why didn't they guard him from pokes and prods and pullings? Then, quite suddenly, he caught sight of somebody, and stiffened all over.

Surely, SURELY, that was one of the men who had taken his father's car? Peter stared and stared. Was it? Oh, why didn't he stand a bit nearer so that he could see?

[16]

The two men

The man was standing by the window of the café, as if he were waiting for someone. He had on a hat and his hair was rather long. Peter looked as closely at him as he could.

The man who drove the car had a low-brimmed hat, he thought, and long hair. This man somehow *looks* like that man we saw in the car.

The man moved a little nearer, and coughed impatiently. He took a handkerchief from his pocket and blew his nose. The top of one middle finger was missing. Peter knew for *certain* that it was the man he was looking for! It *must* be the man! Perhaps he's waiting for the other man.

Almost before he had finished thinking

this, the second man came up! There was no mistaking that cap and the short, cropped hair, grown a little longer now. The cap was pulled down over his face exactly as it had been when he was in the car. He wore an old mac, and Peter tried to see if it had a button missing.

The two men said a word of greeting and then went into the café. They went right through the room to a door at the back, opened it, and disappeared.

'Colin! George! Jack! Those were the two men,' called Peter in a low voice full of excitement. 'One of them had half a finger missing. I saw it.'

'And the other had a button off his mac!' said Jack. 'I noticed that, though I didn't know he was one of the men we're after! But seeing that I'm in charge of the button now, I'm making a point of looking carefully at every mac I see! I believe our button matches his exactly.'

'Good work!' said Peter. 'Now listen. The next move is very, very important. Two of you must shadow these men. If they separate, you must separate too, and each go after one of them. Colin, you must wheel me home.'

'Right,' said the three, always willing to obey Peter's leadership. He really was very good at this kind of thing.

'Get as close to those men as you can and see if you can hear anything useful,' said Peter. 'And track them right to their homes if you can. Report to me at the Secret Seven shed as soon as you can.'

'Right,' said George and Jack, feeling as if they were first-class plain-clothes policemen!

The two men were not long in Sid's. They came out after about ten minutes, looking angry. They stood in the doorway, taking no notice of the Guy and the boys.

'Sid's let us down,' said the man with the

missing finger. 'He said he'd give us two hundred and now he's knocked it down to fifty. Better go back to Q's and tell him. He'll be wild.'

The boys listened intently, pretending to fiddle about with the Guy.

'I'm not arguing with Sid again,' said the other man. 'I reckon I'm an idiot to come out of hiding, yet, till my hair's grown. Come on, let's go.'

They went off down the street, and George and Jack immediately set off behind them, leaving Colin with Peter.

'Did you hear that?' said Peter, in great excitement, forgetting he was a Guy. 'They've stolen something and want to sell it to Sid, and he won't give them what he promised. So they're going back to Q, whoever he is, probably the chief, to report it. Well we know that Q is a man, now!'

'And did you hear what the other man said about his hair growing?' said Colin, bending over Peter. 'I bet he's just come out of prison, it's so short. They always shave it there, don't they? Or perhaps he's an *escaped* prisoner, in hiding. Gosh, Peter, this is super!'

'Wheel me to our shed,' commanded Peter, wishing he could get out and walk. 'Hurry up. The girls will be there already, and George and Jack will join us as soon as they can. Do hurry up! . . . I'm going to get out and walk,' announced Peter. 'It's a nice dark road we're in. Stop a minute, Colin, and I'll get out.'

Colin stopped, and Peter climbed out of the barrow. Colin shone his torch to help him, and an old man with a dog saw the Guy stepping out of the barrow. He stared as if he couldn't believe his eyes, and then hurried off at top speed. Good gracious! A Guy coming alive. No, surely his eyes must have deceived him!

It wasn't long before Colin and Peter

were whispering the password outside the shed at the bottom of Peter's garden. The barrow was shoved into some bushes, and Peter had taken off his mask.

'Bonfire!' said the boys, and the door opened at once. Pam gave a little scream as Peter came in, still looking very peculiar with a black wool wig, an old hat, and very ragged clothes.

'We've got news!' said Peter. 'Great news. Just listen, all of you!'

[17]

Good work!

Peter quickly told the girls all that had happened, and they listened in silence, feeling very thrilled. Now they were really finding out something, even that button had helped!

'I think the short-haired man has either just come out of prison or escaped from it,' said Peter. 'He may have committed a robbery before he went in, and have hidden what he stole, and it's these goods he and the other man are trying to sell to Sid.'

'Well, who's Q, then?' asked Janet. 'Where does *he* come in?'

'He's probably holding the stolen goods,' said Peter, working everything out in his mind. 'And I expect he's sheltering the thief, too. If only we could find out who Q is and where he lives. He's the missing link.'

The five of them talked and talked, and Scamper listened and joined in with a few wuffs now and again, thumping his tail on the ground when the chatter got very loud.

'When will George and Jack be back?' asked Pam. 'I ought not to be too late home, and it's a quarter past six now!'

'Here they are!' said Colin, hearing voices outside. A knock came at the door.

'Password!' shouted everyone.

'Bonfire!' said two voices, and in went George and Jack, beaming all over their faces, glad to be out of the cold, dark November night.

'What happened? Did you shadow them?' demanded Peter, as they sat down on boxes.

'Yes,' said George. 'We followed them all the way down the street, and away by the canal and up by Cole Square. We only once got near enough to hear them say anything.'

'What was that?' asked Peter.

'One of them said "Is that a policeman lying in wait for us over there? Come on, run for it!" ' said George. 'And just as a bobby came out of the shadows they ran round the corner, and the policeman never even noticed them! We shot after them, just in time to see them trying the handles of some cars parked there.'

'Then they slid quickly into one and drove off,' finished Jack. 'That was the end of our shadowing.'

'So they stole *another* car!' said Colin.

'You didn't take the number by any chance, did you?' asked Peter.

'Of course!' said Jack, and took out his notebook. 'Here it is, PLK 100. We didn't go back and tell the policeman. We thought we'd race back here and let you decide what we ought to do next.'

'Good work,' said Peter, pleased. 'If only we knew where Q lived, we'd know where the men were, and could tell the police to go and grab them there. They'd get the stolen goods too. I bet they're being held by our mysterious Q!'

'I know! I know!' suddenly yelled Pam, making everyone jump. 'Why can't we look up all the names beginning with Q in our local telephone directory? If Q lives somewhere here, his name would be there, and his number.'

'Yes but there might be a lot of Qs, and we wouldn't know which was the right one,' objected Janet. 'Why, we ourselves know a Mrs Queen, a Mr Quigley and a Miss Quorn.'

'But don't you see what I *mean*!' said Pam, impatiently. 'We'll go down all the list of Qs, and the one with the telephone number of 8061 will be *our* Q! Don't you *see*?'

Everyone saw what she meant at once.

Peter looked at Pam admiringly. 'That's a very good idea, Pam,' he said. 'I've sometimes thought that you're not as good a Secret Seven member as the others are, but now I know you are. That's a Very Good Idea. Why didn't we think of it before instead of messing about with KEW?'

'I'll get our telephone directory with all the numbers in,' said Janet and raced off.

She soon came back, gave the password and joined the others. She opened the book at the Qs, and everyone craned to look at them.

There were not very many. 'Quant,' read Pam, 'telephone number 6015. Queen, 6453, Quelling, 4322, Quentin, 8061 . . .! That's it. Look, here it is, Quentin, 8061, Barr's Warehouse, East End. Why, that's only about two miles away, right at the other end of the town.'

'Gosh!' said Peter, delighted. 'That's given us JUST the information we wanted. A warehouse, too. A fine place for hiding stolen goods! My goodness, we've done some excellent work. Pam, you deserve a pat on the back!'

She got plenty of pats, and sat back, beaming. 'What do we do now?' she said.

Before anyone could answer, there came the sound of footsteps down the path, and Peter's mother's voice called loudly: 'Peter! Janet! Are Colin and George there, and Pam? Their mothers have just telephoned to say they really must come home at once, it's getting late!'

'Okay!' called Peter. 'Wait for us. We've got a wonderful tale to tell you! Do wait!'

But his mother had gone scurrying back to the house, not liking the cold, damp evening. The seven children tore after her, with Scamper barking his head off.

Just as they went in at the back of the house, there came a knock at the front door.

'See who that is, Peter!' called his mother. 'I've got a cake in the oven I must look at.'

Peter went to the door, with the others close behind him. A big policeman stood there. He smiled at the surprised children.

'I've just been to Jack's house,' he said, 'and Susie told me he might be here. I saw you tonight in Cole Square – you and this other boy here. Well, not long after that somebody reported to me that their car had been stolen near where you were, and I wondered if either of you had noticed anything suspicious going on.'

'Oh, come in, come in!' cried Peter, joyfully. 'We can tell you a whole lot about the thieves, and we can even tell you where you'll probably find the car. Come in, do!'

[18]

Don't worry, Secret Seven!

The policeman went into the hall, looking extremely surprised. Peter's mother came from the kitchen and Peter's father looked out of his study.

'What's all this?' he said. 'Nobody has got into trouble, surely?'

'No,' said Peter. 'Oh, Daddy, you must just listen to our tale. It's really super!'

They all went into the study, the policeman looking more and more puzzled.

'I *think* you'll find that stolen car outside Barr's Warehouse, at the East End of the town,' said Peter. 'And in the warehouse you'll probably find a Mr Quentin, and quite a lot of stolen goods on the premises.'

'And you'll find a man with half a finger

missing, and another whose hair is so short that he looks like an escaped prisoner,' put in Colin.

'Wait! Wait a minute! What's this about a man with a missing half-finger?' said the policeman, urgently. 'We're looking for him – Fingers, he's called, and he's a friend of a thief who's just been in prison. He escaped last week, and we thought he might go to Fingers for help, so we've been keeping an eye open for him too.'

'They met at Sid's Café,' said Peter, enjoying everyone's astonishment.

'WHAT?' said his father. 'Sid's Café? That horrible place! Don't dare to tell me you boys have been in there.'

'Not inside, only outside,' said Peter. 'It's all right, we *really* haven't done anything wrong. It all began with that night when you left Janet and me in your car in the station yard, and two men got in and drove it away.'

'And we wanted you to go to the police, but you didn't think you'd bother,' said Janet. 'So we've been trying to trace the two men ourselves, and we have!'

Then the whole of the story came out how they found Sid's Café, how Peter dressed up as a Guy to watch for the men, how they saw Fingers with his missing half-finger, and how George and Jack followed them and saw them steal the car near Cole Square.

'And we know where they've gone, because they have a friend called Q, a Mr Quentin,' said Peter. 'They mentioned his telephone number, it was 8061, and we looked up the number and found the address. We only did that a little while ago, actually. The address is Barr's Warehouse, as we said.'

'Amazing!' said the policeman, scribbling fast in his notebook. 'Incredible! Do these kids do this kind of thing often?'

'Well, you're a fairly new man here,' said Peter's father, 'or you'd know how they keep poking their noses into all sorts of things. I don't know that I really approve of it, but they certainly have done some good work.'

'We're the Secret Seven Society, you see,' explained Janet. 'And we really do like some kind of adventurous job to do.'

'Well, thanks very much,' said the policeman, getting up. 'I'll get a few men and ask the Sergeant to come along with us and see what we can find in Barr's Warehouse. You'll deserve a jolly good Bonfire Night tomorrow! I hope you've got a wonderful collection of fireworks, you deserve the best!'

'Our families are joining together for a big bonfire party. We all saved up for the fireworks and Colin's father is keeping them for us – though I expect all our fathers will take turns letting them off!'

'Well, have a good evening then – and mind you all take care not to get too close!' said the policeman, going to the door. 'I'm much obliged to you all. Good night!'

'What a tale!' said Peter's mother. 'I never heard of such goings-on! Whatever will you Seven do next? To think of you dressing up as a Guy, Peter, and watching outside Sid's Café! No wonder you look SO DREADFUL! Take that black wig off, do!'

'*Can't* the others stay and have a bit of supper?' Peter begged her. 'We've got such a lot to talk about. Do let them. Sandwiches will do. We'll all help to make them.'

'Very well,' said his mother, laughing at all the excited faces. 'Janet, go and telephone everybody's mothers and tell them where they are!'

The Seven were very pleased. In fifteen minutes' time they were all sitting down to potted meat sandwiches, oatmeal biscuits, apples and hot cocoa, talking nineteen to the dozen, with a very excited Scamper tearing round their legs under the table. What an unexpected party! thought Scamper, delighted, and what a wonderful selection of titbits!

The telephone suddenly rang, and Peter went to answer it. It proved to be a very exciting call indeed! He came racing back to the others.

'That was that policeman! He thought we'd like to know what happened.'

'What? Tell us!' cried everyone.

'Well, the police went to Barr's Warehouse and the first thing they saw in the yard was the stolen car!' said Peter. 'Then they forced their way in at the back door, and found Mr Quentin, scared stiff, in his office. When they told him they knew that Fingers and the escaped prisoner were somewhere in the warehouse, he just crumpled up!'

'Have they got the others?' asked Colin.

'Oh yes. Quentin showed the police where they were hiding,' said Peter. 'Down in a cellar, and the stolen goods were there too. It was a wonderful raid! By the way, the police want to know if we can identify the second man, the close-cropped man, and I said yes, if he was wearing a mac with a missing button, because we've got the button!'

'Goody, goody!' said Barbara. 'So we have. We forgot to tell the policeman about that! Where *is* the button?'

'Here,' said Jack, and spun it on the table. 'Good old button, you did your bit too! Gosh, this is one of the most exciting jobs the Secret Seven have ever done. I'm jolly sorry it's ended.'

So was everyone. They didn't want that exciting evening to come to a finish, but they had to say goodbye at last.

'Tomorrow is Bonfire Night,' said Peter to Janet as they shut the front door on the others. 'We'll all have a wonderful party and Colin's Guy will look down on us all from the top of the bonfire.'

'Shall we put you there instead, Peter? You'd look even better!' said Janet, smiling.

'I'd much rather watch the Guy than be him tomorrow night,' said Peter, 'though it was exciting being a Guy just for one night! Come on, Janet, let's go up to bed and dream about all those super fireworks . . .'

They both ran upstairs shouting at the tops of their voices, 'Bang! Whoosh! Bang-Bang-Bang!'

If you can't wait
to read more about
THE SECRET SEVEN,
then turn over for
the beginning of their
next adventure...

SECRET
SEVEN
WIN THROUGH

[1]

The holidays begin

'Easter holidays at last!' said Peter. 'I thought they were never coming. Didn't you, Janet?'

'Yes. It was a dreadfully long term,' said Janet. 'We've broken up now though, thank goodness. Don't you love the first day of the hols, Peter?'

'You bet! I get a lovely *free* sort of feeling,' said Peter, 'and the hols seem to stretch out in front of me for ages and ages. Let's have some fun, Janet!'

'Yes, let's! April's a lovely month – it's warm, and sunny too, and Mummy will let us off on picnics any day we like,' said Janet. 'Scamper, do you hear that? Picnics, I said – and that means rabbit-hunting for you, and long, long walks.'

'Woof!' said Scamper at once, his tail thumping on the floor, and his eyes bright.

'You're the best and finest golden spaniel in the whole world!' said Janet, stroking his silky head. 'And I do so love your long, droopy ears, Scamper. You like it when we have holidays, don't you?'

'Woof!' said Scamper again, and thump-thump-thump went his tail.

'I vote we have a meeting of the Secret Seven as soon as we can,' said Peter. 'To-morrow, if possible. Picnics and things are much more fun if we all go together.'

'Yes. Let's have a meeting,' said Janet. 'What with exams and one thing and an-other all the Secret Seven have forgotten about the Society. I haven't thought a word about it for at least three weeks. Gosh – what's the password?'

'Oh, Janet – you haven't forgotten that *surely*?' said Peter.

'You tell me,' said Janet, but Peter wouldn't. 'You don't know it yourself!' said Janet. 'I bet you don't!'

'Don't be silly,' said Peter. 'You'll have to remember it by tomorrow, if we have a meeting! Where's your badge? I expect you've lost that.'

'I have *not*,' said Janet. 'But I bet some of the others will have lost theirs. Somebody always does when we don't have a meeting for some time.'

'Better write out short notes to the other five,' said Peter, 'and tell them to come along tomorrow. Got some notepaper, Janet?'

'Yes, I have. But I don't feel a bit like sitting down and writing the first day of the hols,' said Janet. 'You can jolly well help to write them.'

'No. I'll bike round to all the others and deliver the notes for you,' said Peter.

'Now it's *you* who are silly,' said Janet. 'If you're going to everyone's house, why not *tell* them about the meeting. All this note-writing! You just *tell* them.'

'All right. It just seems more *official* if we send out notes for a meeting, that's all,' said Peter. 'What time shall we have it?'

'Oh, half-past ten, I should think,' said Janet. 'And just warn Jack that he's not to let his horrid sister Susie know, or she'll come banging at the door, shouting out some silly password at the top of her voice.'

'Yes. I'll tell him,' said Peter. 'The worst of it is, Susie is so jolly sharp. She always seems to smell out anything to do with the Secret Seven.'

'She would be a better person to have *in* a club than out of it,' said Janet. 'But we'll never, never let her into ours.'

'Never,' said Peter. 'Anyway, we can't be more than seven, or we wouldn't be the Secret Seven.'

'Woof!' said Scamper.

'He says he belongs, even if we're seven and he makes the eighth!' said Janet. 'You're just a hanger-on, Scamper, but we simply couldn't do without you.'

'Well, I'm going to get my bike,' said Peter, getting up. 'I'll go round and tell all the others. See you later, Janet. Coming, Scamper?'

Off he went, and was soon cycling to one house after another. He went to Colin first, who was delighted to hear the news.

'Good!' he said. 'Half-past ten? Right, I'll be there. I say – whatever's the password, Peter?'

'You've got all day to think of it!' said Peter, with a grin, and rode off to Jack's. Jack was in the garden, mending a puncture in the back wheel of his bicycle. He was very pleased to see Peter.

'Meeting of the Secret Seven tomorrow morning in the shed at the bottom of our garden,' said Peter. 'I hope you've got your badge, and that your awful sister Susie hasn't found it and taken it.'

'I've got it on,' said Jack, with a grin. 'And I wear it on my pyjamas at night, so it's always safe. I say, Peter – what's the password?'

'*I* can tell you!' said a voice from up a near-by tree. The boys looked up to see Susie's laughing face looking down at them.

'You don't know it!' said Jack fiercely.

'I do, I do!' said the annoying Susie. 'But I shan't tell you, and you won't be allowed in at the meeting. What a joke!'

Peter rode off to the rest of the Seven. That Susie! She really was the most AGGRAVATING girl in the whole world

Pocket Guide to Basic Dysrhythmias

interpretation & management

Robert J. Huszar, M.D.
Former Medical Director
Emergency Medical Services Program
New York State Department of Health

with 145 illustrations

St. Louis Baltimore Berlin Boston Carlsbad Chicago London Madrid
Naples New York Philadelphia Sydney Tokyo Toronto

Dedicated to Publishing Excellence

Publisher: **David T. Culverwell**
Executive Editor: **Richard A. Weimer**
Editorial Project Supervisor: **Cecilia F. Reilly**
Assistant Editor: **Jennifer Roe**
Project Manager: **Dana Peick**
Production Editor: **Catherine Albright**
Manufacturing Supervisor: **Karen Lewis**

Printed in the United States of America
Film separation by Accu-Color, Inc.
Printing/binding by R.R. Donnelley & Sons, Co.

Mosby-Year Book, Inc.
11830 Westline Industrial Drive
St. Louis, Missouri 63146

ISBN 0-8151-4746-5
25902

95 96 97 98 99   9 8 7 6 5 4 3 2

Preface

The **Pocket Guide to Basic Dysrhythmias** is intended to be used as a pocket reference in the interpretation of arrhythmias; bundle branch and fascicular blocks; miscellaneous ECG changes (such as occur in chamber enlargement, pericarditis, electrolyte imbalance, drug administration, and pulmonary disease); and ECG patterns in acute myocardial infarction. The interpretation of arrhythmias and some of the miscellaneous ECG changes rely on the analysis of a single ECG lead, usually lead II, while the identification of bundle branch and fascicular blocks, acute myocardial infarction, and the rest of the miscellaneous ECG changes rely on the analysis of the 12-lead ECG.

The pocket guide also includes basic information on the electrical conduction system of the heart and its coronary circulation; the placement of leads in a monitoring ECG lead II, a monitoring ECG lead MCL_1, and a 12-lead ECG; the derivation of the hexaxial reference figure, the lead axes and their perpendiculars, and the normal and abnormal QRS axes; the three-lead method of determining the QRS axis; the components of the electrocardiogram; and the steps in interpreting the ECG and the methods of determining the heart rate.

And, finally, the pocket guide includes a section on the treatment of arrhythmias, based on the recommendations of the **1992 National Conference on Standards and Guidelines for Cardiopulmonary Resuscitation (CPR) and Emergency Cardiac Care (ECC)** sponsored by the **American College of Cardiology,** the **American Heart Association,** the **American Red Cross,** and the **National Heart, Lung and Blood Institute.**

The **Pocket Guide to Basic Dysrhythmias** is also intended to complement **Basic Dysrhythmias, second edition** from which the text, illustrations, and electrocardiograms were abstracted and then modified to some extent by the author. **Micrografx Designer 4.1** was used in preparing the illustrations and electrocardiograms for the pocket guide, and **PageMaker 5.0,** the layout of the pages and the book. I wish to acknowledge the assistance of Marta Huszar in designing the front and back covers.

A Note to the Reader

The author and publisher have made every attempt to check dosages and advanced life support content for accuracy. The care procedures presented here represent accepted practices in the United States. They are not offered as a standard of care. Advanced life support level emergency care is performed under the authority of a licensed physician. It is the reader's responsibility to know and follow local care protocols as provided by their medical advisers. It is also the reader's responsibility to stay informed of emergency care procedure changes.

This book is dedicated
to my wife, Jean

Contents

LIST OF CREDITS

The following art work was borrowed from:
Huszar, Robert J.: *Basic Dysrhythmias Interpretation and Management,* ed 2, St. Louis, 1994, Mosby.

Pages 42-45, 47, 50, 52, 62-64, 68, 69, 72, 74-76, 78, 80, 82, 84, 88, 90-93.

All other art in this pocket guide was adapted from:
Huszar, Robert J.: *Basic Dysrhythmias Interpretation and Management,* ed 2, St. Louis, 1994, Mosby.

Section I

Arrhythmia Identification

Normal Sinus Rhythm (NSR)

Lead II

Heart Rate: **60-100/min.**

Rhythm: Essentially **regular.**

Pacemaker Site: **SA node.**

P Waves: Upright in lead II; identical and precede each QRS complex.

PR Intervals: **Normal (0.12-0.20 sec); constant.**

R-R Intervals: **Equal.**

QRS Complexes: Usually **normal (0.10 sec or less),** unless a preexisting intraventricular conduction disturbance[1] is present.

[1]The most common form of **intraventricular conduction disturbance** is a **right** or **left bundle branch block;** a less common form is a nonspecific, diffuse **intraventricular conduction defect (IVCD)** seen in myocardial infarction, fibrosis, and hypertrophy; electrolyte imbalance, such as hypo- and hyperkalemia; and excessive administration of such cardiac drugs as quinidine and procainamide.

Treatment: None.

Sinus Arrhythmia

Heart Rate: **60-100/min.** Typically, the heart rate increases during inspiration and decreases during expiration.

Rhythm: Regularly **irregular.**

Pacemaker Site: **SA node.**

P Waves: Upright in lead II; identical and precede each QRS complex.

PR Intervals: **Normal (0.12-0.20 sec); constant.**

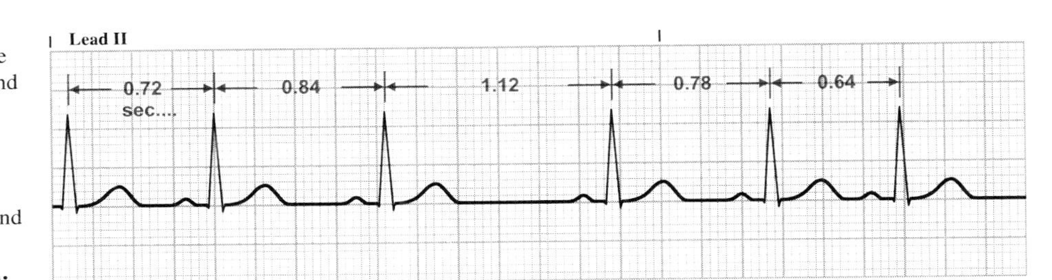

R-R Intervals: **Unequal;** shorter during inspiration, longer during expiration.

QRS Complexes: Usually **normal (0.10 sec or less),** unless a preexisting intraventricular conduction disturbance is present.

Treatment: None.

Sinus Bradycardia

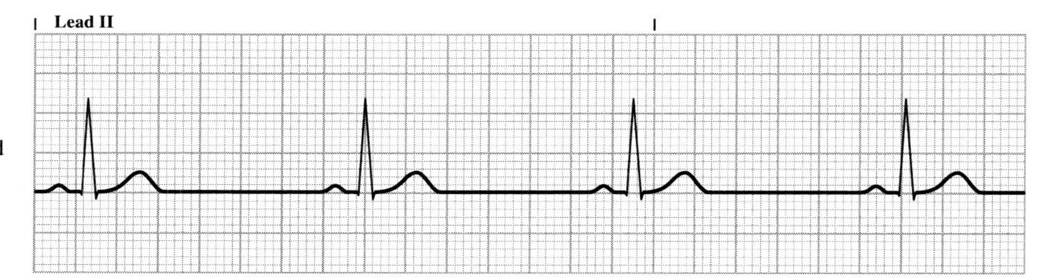

Heart Rate: **Less than 60/min.**

Rhythm: Essentially **regular.**

Pacemaker Site: **SA node.**

P Waves: Upright in lead II; identical and precede each QRS complex.

PR Intervals: **Normal (0.12-0.20 sec); constant.**

R-R Intervals: **Equal.**

QRS Complexes: Usually **normal (0.10 sec or less),** unless a preexisting intraventricular conduction disturbance is present.

Treatment: See page 30, Section II.

Sinus Arrest and Sinoatrial (SA) Exit Block

Lead II

X >3X >2X

sinus arrest

X 3X 2X

sinoatrial (SA) exit block

Heart Rate: **60-100/min** or less.

Rhythm: **Irregular** when sinus arrest or SA exit block is present.

Pacemaker Site: **SA node.**

P Waves: **Absent** when sinus arrest or SA exit block is present **(dropped P wave).**

PR Intervals: **Absent** when sinus arrest or SA exit block is present.

R-R Intervals: **Unequal** when sinus arrest or SA exit block is present.

QRS Complexes: Usually **normal (0.10 sec or less),** unless a preexisting intraventricular conduction disturbance is present.

Treatment: See page 30, Section II.

Sinus Tachycardia

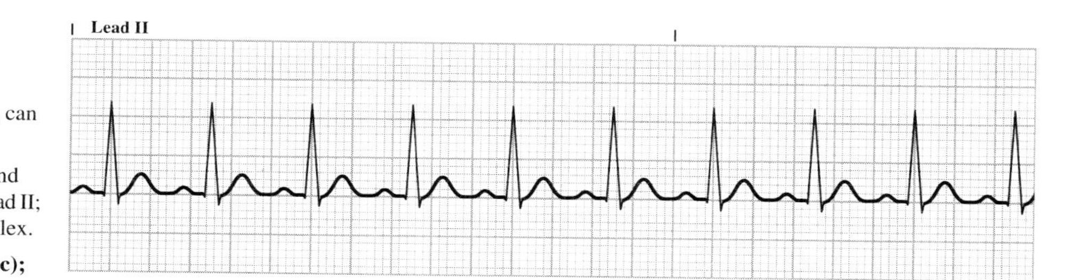

Rhythm: Essentially **regular.**

Pacemaker Site: SA node.

Heart Rate: Greater than 100/min, can be as high as **180/min** or greater.

P Waves: Normal, or slightly taller and more peaked than normal; upright in lead II; identical and precede each QRS complex.

PR Intervals: Normal (0.12-0.20 sec); constant.

R-R Intervals: Usually **equal,** but may be **slightly unequal.**

QRS Complexes: Usually **normal (0.10 sec or less),** unless a preexisting intraventricular conduction disturbance is present.

Treatment: No specific treatment indicated.

Wandering Atrial Pacemaker (WAP)

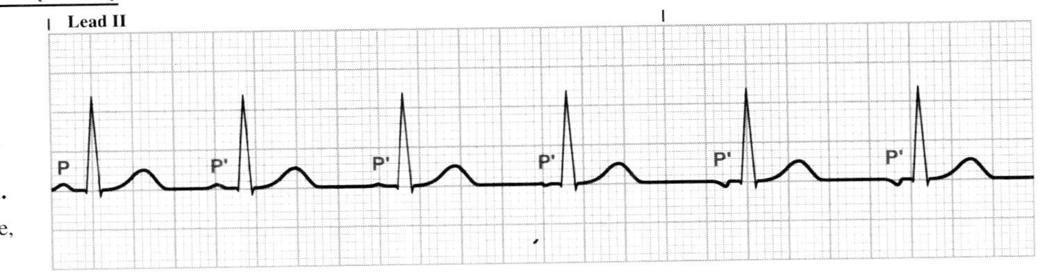

Heart Rate: Usually **60-100/min,** but may be less.

Rhythm: Usually **irregular.**

Pacemaker Site: Shifts back and forth between the **SA node** and an **ectopic pacemaker** in the **atria** or **AV junction.**

P Waves: Gradually change in size, shape, and direction from normal, positive (upright) P waves to abnormally small, even negative (inverted) P´waves over a series of beats, and then back again to normal in a reverse sequence; precede each QRS complex.

PR Intervals: Unequal; varies within **normal limits (0.12-0.20 sec)** from about 0.20 sec to about 0.12 sec over a series of beats and then back again.

R-R Intervals: Usually **unequal.**

QRS Complexes: Usually **normal (0.10 sec or less),** unless a preexisting intraventricular conduction disturbance is present.

Treatment: No specific treatment indicated.

Premature Atrial Contractions (PACs)

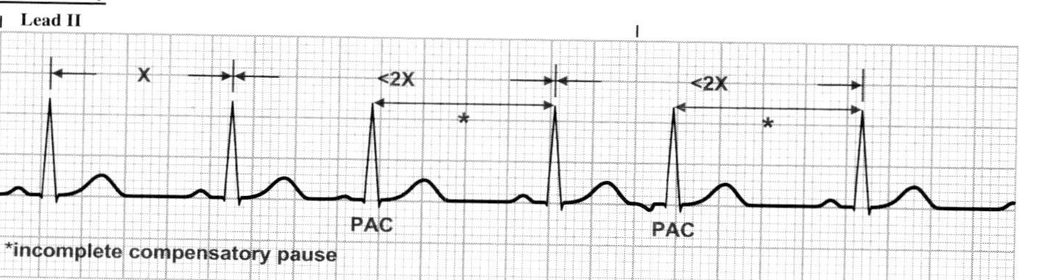

Heart Rate: That of the underlying rhythm.

Rhythm: Irregular when PACs are present.

Pacemaker Site: An **ectopic pacemaker** in the **atria.**

P´Waves: P´waves occur earlier than the next expected P wave of the underlying rhythm. They vary in size, shape, and direction in any given lead depending on the site of their origin. P´waves followed by QRS complexes related to them are **conducted PACs.** P´waves occurring alone, not followed by QRS complexes, are **non-conducted** or **blocked PACs.**

P-P Intervals: The **P-P´ interval** is usually shorter and the **P´-P interval,** the same or slightly longer than the P-P interval of the underlying rhythm. Commonly, an **incomplete compensatory pause** is present, i.e., the sum of the **P-P´** and the **P´-P intervals** is less than twice the P-P interval of the underlying rhythm. Rarely, a **complete compensatory pause** is present, i.e., the sum of the **P-P´**and the **P´-P intervals** is equal to twice the underlying P-P interval.

P´R Intervals: Normal (0.12-0.20 sec); may vary between PACs.

Treatment: See page 32, Section II.

R-R Intervals: Unequal when PACs are present.

QRS Complexes: Usually **normal (0.10 sec or less),** resembling those of the underlying rhythm. If aberrant ventricular conduction[2] is present, the PAC may be wide and bizarre, resembling a PVC—**PAC with aberrancy.**

[2]A temporary delay in the conduction of an electrical impulse through the bundle branches producing an abnormally wide QRS complex, caused by the appearance of the electrical impulse at the bundle branches prematurely while they are still partially refractory and unable to conduct normally. The QRS complex may show a right or left bundle branch block pattern or a combination of a right bundle branch block pattern and a left anterior or posterior fascicular block pattern.

Types of PACs

Infrequent PACs: Less than five PACs/min.

Frequent PACs: Five or more PACs/min.

Isolated PACs (Beats): PACs occurring singly.

Group Beats: PACs occurring in groups of two or more.

Paired PACs (Couplet): Two PACs in a row.

Atrial Tachycardia: Three or more PACs in a row.

Atrial Bigeminy: PACs alternating with the QRS complexes of the underlying rhythm.

Atrial Trigeminy/Atrial Quadrigeminy: PACs following every two or three QRS complexes of the underlying rhythm, respectively.

— = PACs

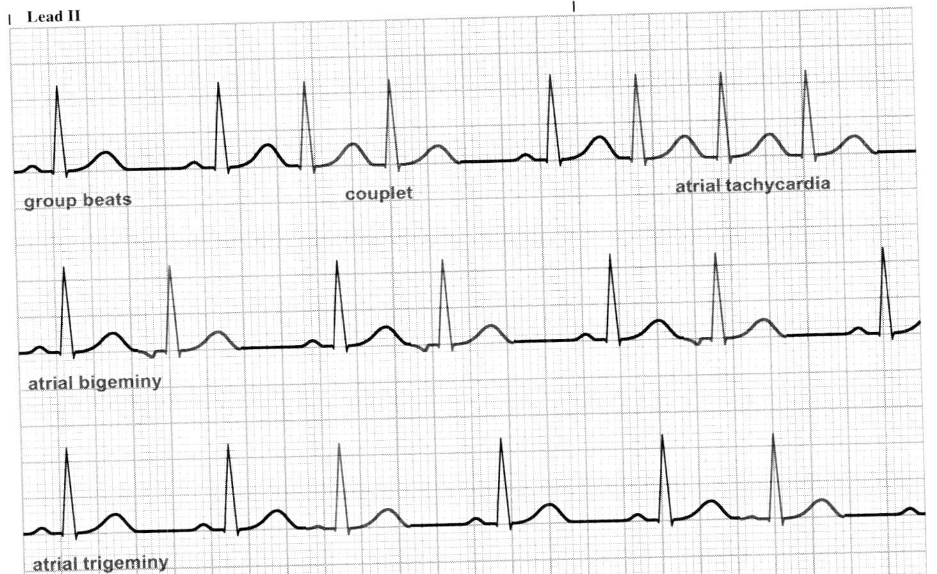

Paroxysmal Supraventricular Tachycardia (PSVT)
Paroxysmal Atrial Tachycardia (PAT), Paroxysmal Junctional Tachycardia (PJT)

Heart Rate: Usually **160-240/min.** **PSVT** occurs in **paroxysms,** beginning abruptly and lasting a few seconds to many hours.

Rhythm: Essentially **regular.**

Pacemaker Site: An **ectopic pacemaker** in the **atria (paroxysmal atrial tachycardia [PAT])** or **AV junction (paroxysmal junctional tachycardia [PJT]).**

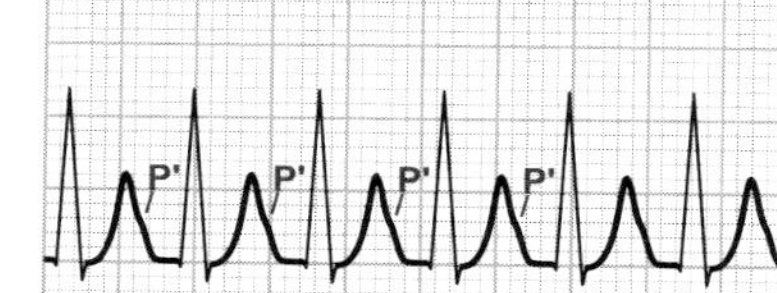

P´Waves: Present or **absent.** When present, the P´waves either precede or follow each QRS complex. The P´waves may be either **(1) positive (upright) in lead II** if they originate in the atria near the SA node or **(2) negative (inverted)** if they originate in the atria near the AV junction or in the AV junction itself. The P´waves are usually **identical** in any given lead. P´waves are absent **(1)** if they occur during the QRS complex or **(2)** if the ectopic pacemaker is in the AV junction and a retrograde AV block is present.

P´R Intervals: If the P´waves precede each QRS complex, the P´R intervals may be **(1) normal (0.12-0.20 sec)** if the ectopic pacemaker is in the atria or **(2) abnormal (less than 0.12 sec)** if the ectopic pacemaker is in the AV junction. If the P´waves follow each QRS complex, the RP´ intervals are **less than 0.20 sec.** The P´R and RP´ intervals are usually **constant.**

Treatment: See pages 33 and 35, Section II.

R-R Intervals: Usually **equal.**

QRS Complexes: Usually **normal (0.10 sec or less),** unless aberrant ventricular conduction, anomalous AV conduction (preexcitation syndrome)[3], or a preexisting intraventricular conduction disturbance is present. If the wide and bizarre QRS complexes occur only with the PSVT, the arrhythmia is called **PSVT with aberrancy** (or **PSVT with aberrant ventricular conduction**). Such a PSVT usually resembles **ventricular tachycardia.**

[3]Abnormal conduction of electrical impulses from the atria to the ventricles via an accessory pathway bypassing the AV junction. This commonly results in a shorter than normal PR interval **(0.09-0.12 sec)** and a wide QRS complex **(0.10 sec or more)** with an initial slurring of the upward slope of the R wave (the **delta wave**), all of which is characteristic of the **Wolff-Parkinson-White (WPW) syndrome.**

Atrial Flutter

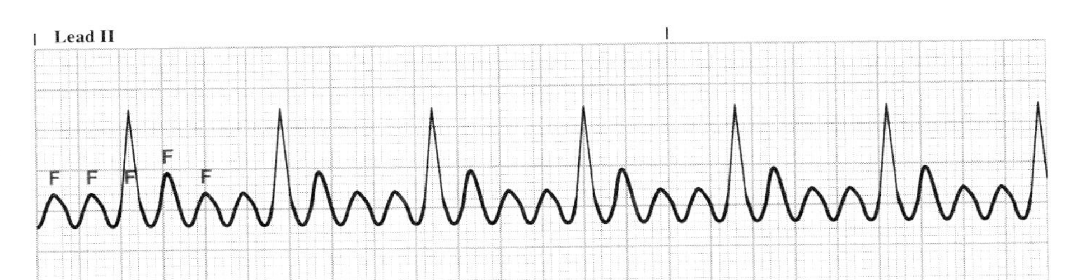

Heart Rate: Atrial rate: 240-360 (average, 300) F waves/min.

Ventricular rate: Usually about **150/min** if atrial flutter is uncontrolled (untreated); **60-75/min** if controlled (treated) or if a preexisting AV block is present.

Rhythm: Usually **regular,** but may be **irregular.**

Pacemaker Site: An **ectopic pacemaker** in the **atria.**

F Waves: Identical **saw-toothed shaped repetitive waves.**

FR Intervals: Usually **equal,** but may be **unequal.**

R-R Intervals: Usually **equal** and **constant,** but may be **unequal.**

QRS Complexes: Usually **normal (0.10 sec or less),** unless aberrant ventricular conduction, anomalous AV conduction, or a preexisting intraventricular conduction disturbance is present.

Treatment: See page 34, Section II.

Atrial Fibrillation (AF)

Lead II

f f f f f f f f f

Heart Rate: **Atrial rate: 350-600 or more (average, 400) f waves/min.**

Ventricular rate: Usually **160-180/min** if atrial fibrillation is uncontrolled (untreated); **60-70/min** if controlled (treated) or if a preexisting AV block is present.

Rhythm: **Irregularly (grossly) irregular.**

Pacemaker Site: Multiple **ectopic pacemakers** in the **atria.**

f Waves: Irregularly shaped, rounded (or pointed), and dissimilar **atrial fibrillation (f) waves.** If the f waves are large **(≥1 mm), "coarse" fibrillatory waves** are present; if they are small **(<1 mm), "fine" fibrillatory waves** are present.

fR Intervals: None.

R-R Intervals: Typically **unequal.**

QRS Complexes: Usually **normal (0.10 sec or less),** unless aberrant ventricular conduction, anomalous AV conduction, or a preexisting intraventricular conduction disturbance is present.

Treatment: See page 34, Section II.

Junctional Escape Rhythm

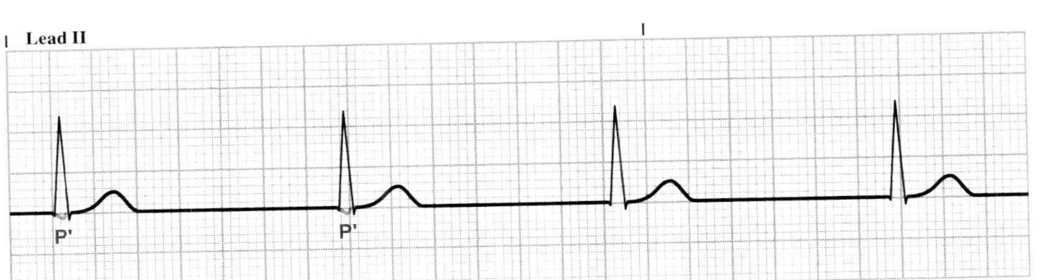

Heart Rate: **40-60/min,** but may be less.

Rhythm: Essentially **regular.**

Pacemaker Site: An **escape pacemaker** in the **AV junction.**

P´Waves: P waves may be present or absent. If present, they either **(1)** regularly precede or follow each QRS complex, in which case, they are negative (inverted) in lead II (P´waves), or **(2)** occur independently, usually being positive (upright) in lead II. If the P waves occur independently of the QRS complexes, **atrioventricular (AV) dissociation** is present.

P´R/RP´ Intervals: If the P´waves regularly precede the QRS complexes, the P´R intervals are **abnormal (less than 0.12 sec).** If the P´waves regularly follow the QRS complexes, the RP´ intervals are **less than 0.20 seconds.**

R-R Intervals: Usually **equal.**

QRS Complexes: Usually **normal (0.10 sec or less),** unless a preexisting intraventricular conduction disturbance is present.

Treatment: See page 32, Section II.

Premature Junctional Contractions (PJCs)

no PJC's ontest

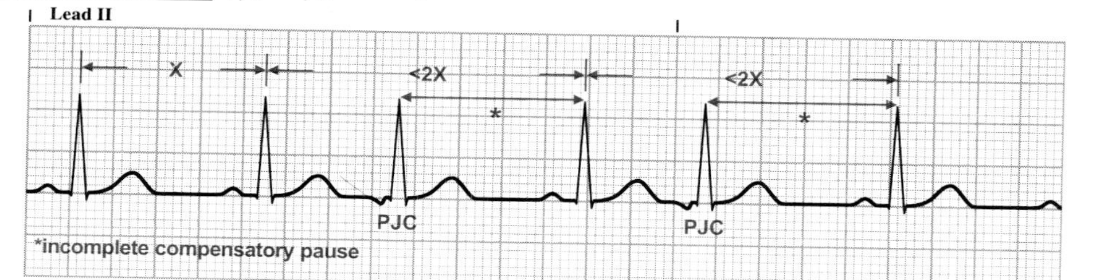

Heart Rate: That of the underlying rhythm.

Rhythm: **Irregular** when PJCs are present.

Pacemaker Site: An **ectopic pacemaker** in the **AV junction.**

P´Waves: **P´waves** may or may not be associated with the PJCs. If present, they usually differ from the P waves of the underlying rhythm in size, shape, and direction. The P´waves are negative (inverted) in lead II. They may precede, be buried in, or, less commonly, follow the QRS complexes of the PJCs. P´waves followed by QRS complexes related to them are **conducted PJCs;** those occurring alone, not followed by QRS complexes, are **nonconducted** or **blocked PJCs.**

P´R/RP´ Intervals: If P´waves regularly precede the QRS complexes of the PJCs, the P´R intervals are **abnormal (less than 0.12 sec).** If P´waves regularly follow the QRS complexes, the RP´ intervals are **less than 0.20 seconds.**

R-R Intervals: **Unequal** when PJCs are present. The **pre-PJC R-R interval** is shorter and the **post-PJC R-R interval** longer than the R-R interval of the underlying rhythm. Commonly, a **complete compensatory pause** is present, i.e., the sum of the **pre-** and **post-PJC R-R intervals** is twice the **R-R interval** of the underlying rhythm. When the sum is less than twice the R-R interval of the underlying rhythm (uncommonly), an **incomplete compensatory** (or **noncompensatory**) **pause** is present.

QRS Complexes: The QRS complexes of the PJCs occur earlier than the next expected QRS complex of the underlying rhythm. Usually they are **normal (0.10 sec or less),** resembling those of the underlying rhythm. If aberrant ventricular conduction is present, the PJC may be wide and bizarre, resembling a PVC: **PJC with aberrancy.**

Treatment: See page 32, Section II.

Types of PJCs

Infrequent PJCs: Less than five PJCs/min.

Frequent PJCs: Five or more PJCs/min.

Isolated PJCs (Beats): PJCs occurring singly.

Group Beats: PJCs occurring in groups of two or more.

Paired PJCs (Couplet): Two PJCs in a row.

Junctional Tachycardia: Three or more PJCs in a row.

Junctional Bigeminy: PJCs alternating with the QRS complexes of the underlying rhythm.

Junctional Trigeminy/Quadrigeminy: PJCs following every two or three QRS complexes of the underlying rhythm, respectively.

— = PJCs

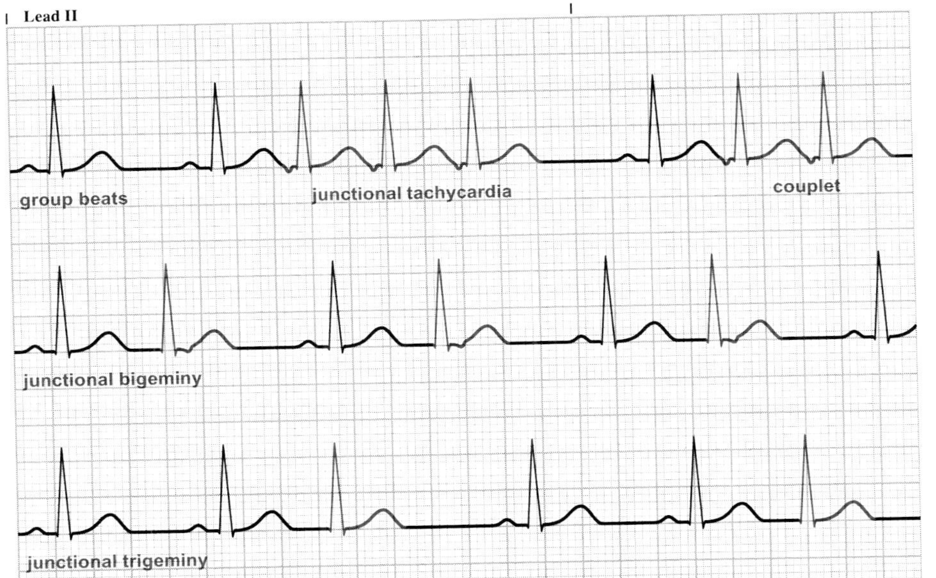

Nonparoxysmal Junctional Tachycardia
(Accelerated Junctional Rhythm, Junctional Tachycardia)

Heart Rate: Usually **60-130/min,** but may be as high as **150/min. Accelerated junctional rhythm: 60-100/min. Junctional tachycardia: 100/min** or greater. Onset and termination are usually gradual.

Lead II

P' P' P'

Rhythm: Essentially **regular.**

Pacemaker Site: An **ectopic pacemaker** in the **AV junction.**

P Waves: P waves may be present or absent. When present, they either **(1)** regularly precede or follow each QRS complex, in which case, they are negative (inverted) in lead II (P´waves), or **(2)** occur independently, in which case, they are either positive (upright) or negative (inverted) in lead II. When the P waves occur independently of the QRS complexes, **atrioventricular (AV) dissociation** is present.

P´R/RP´ Intervals: If P´waves regularly precede the QRS complexes, the P´R intervals are **abnormal (less than 0.12 sec).** If P´waves regularly follow the QRS complexes, the RP´intervals are **less than 0.20 seconds.**

R-R Intervals: Usually **equal.**

QRS Complexes: Usually **normal (0.10 sec or less),** unless aberrant ventricular conduction or a preexisting intraventricular conduction disturbance is present.

Treatment: No specific treatment indicated.

Accelerated Idioventricular Rhythm (AIVR)

Lead II

Heart Rate: 40-100/min.

Rhythm: Regular, but may be **irregular.**

Pacemaker Site: An **ectopic pacemaker** in the **ventricles.**

P Waves: P waves may be present or absent. If present, they are usually of the underlying rhythm and bear no relation to the QRS complexes, sometimes appearing here and there as notches on the QRS complexes, ST segments and T waves. Uncommonly, negative P´waves related to the arrhythmia regularly follow the QRS complexes.

RP´ Intervals: Present if P´waves regularly follow the QRS complexes; **about 0.20 second or less.**

R-R Intervals: Usually **equal,** but may be **slightly unequal.**

QRS Complexes: Typically, **wide (0.12 sec or greater) and bizarre.** Usually identical but may vary slightly.

Treatment: Usually no specific treatment indicated.

Ventricular Escape Rhythm

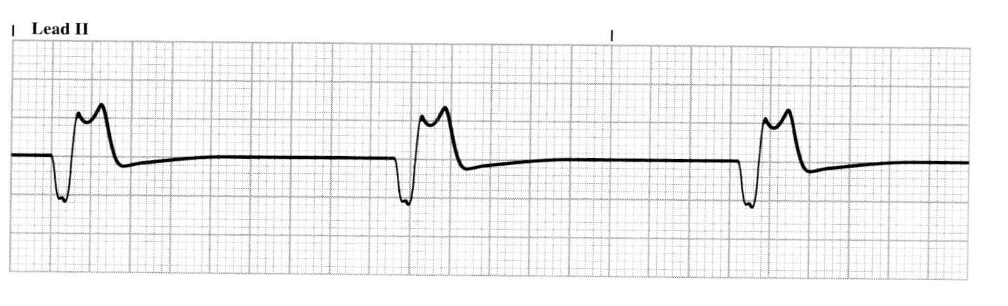

Heart Rate: Usually **30-40/min,** but may be less.

Rhythm: **Regular,** but may be **irregular.**

Pacemaker Site: An **escape pacemaker** in the **ventricles.**

P Waves: P waves may be present or absent. If present, they are usually of the underlying rhythm and bear no relation to the QRS complexes, marching between and through them.

P´R/RP´ Intervals: None.

R-R Intervals: Usually **equal,** but may be **slightly unequal.**

QRS Complexes: Typically, **wide (0.12 sec or greater) and bizarre.** Usually identical, but may vary slightly.

Treatment: See page 32, Section II.

Ventricular Asystole

Heart Rate: None.

Rhythm: None.

Pacemaker Site: None.

P Waves: P waves may be present or absent.

PR Intervals: None.

R-R Intervals: None.

QRS Complexes: None.

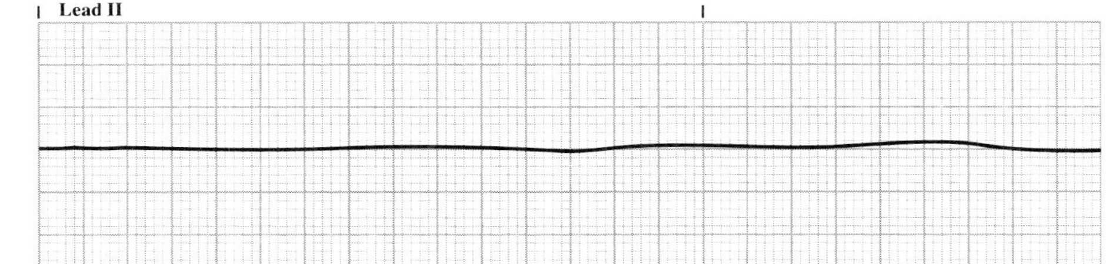

Treatment: See page 38, Section II.

Premature Ventricular Contractions (PVCs)

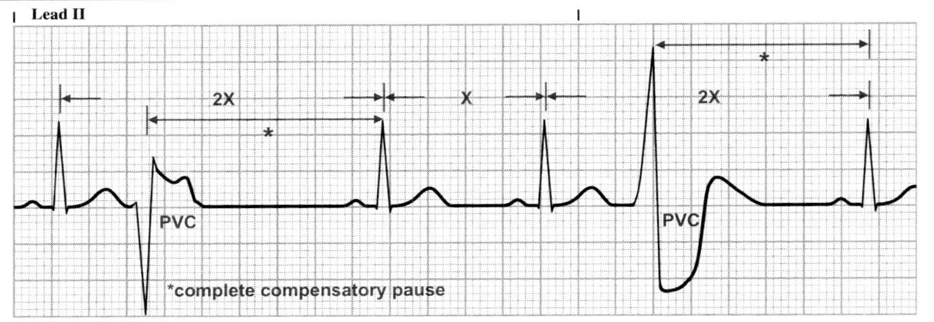

Heart Rate: That of the underlying rhythm.

Rhythm: Irregular when PVCs are present.

Pacemaker Site: An **ectopic pacemaker** in the **ventricles.**

P Waves: P waves may be present or absent. If present, they are usually of the underlying rhythm and bear no relation to the PVCs, sometimes appearing as notches in the QRS complex, ST segment, or T wave of the PVCs. Uncommonly, negative P´waves related to the PVCs regularly follow the QRS complexes of the PVCs.

RP´ Intervals: Present if P´waves occur with the PVCs, typically following them; **about 0.20 second or less.**

R-R Intervals: **Unequal** when PVCs are present. The **coupling interval,** the interval between the PVC and the preceding QRS complex of the underlying rhythm, is shorter and the **post-PVC R-R interval,** longer than the R-R interval of the underlying rhythm. Commonly, a **complete compensatory pause** is present, i.e., the sum of the **coupling interval** and the **post-PVC R-R interval** is twice the **R-R interval** of the underlying rhythm. Rarely, when the sum is less than twice the R-R interval of the underlying rhythm, an **incomplete compensatory pause** is present.

QRS Complexes: Typically, **wide (0.12 sec or greater) and bizarre.** Identical PVCs with the same coupling intervals are **unifocal or uniform PVCs.** Differing PVCs with the same coupling intervals are **multiform PVCs.** PVCs with different QRS complexes and varying coupling intervals are **multifocal PVCs.**

Treatment: See page 35, Section II.

Types of PVCs

Infrequent PVCs: Less than five PVCs/min.

Frequent PVCs: Five or more PVCs/min.

Isolated PVCs (Beats): PVCs occurring singly.

Group Beats, Bursts, Salvos: PVCs occurring in groups of two or more.

Paired PVCs (Couplet): Two PVCs in a row.

Ventricular Tachycardia: Three or more PVCs in a row.

Ventricular Bigeminy: PVCs alternating with the QRS complexes of the underlying rhythm.

Ventricular Trigeminy/Ventricular Quadrigeminy: PVCs following every two or three QRS complexes of the underlying rhythm, respectively.

R-on-T Phenomenon: A PVC occurring during the peak of the T wave (vulnerable period of ventricular repolarization).

— = PVCs

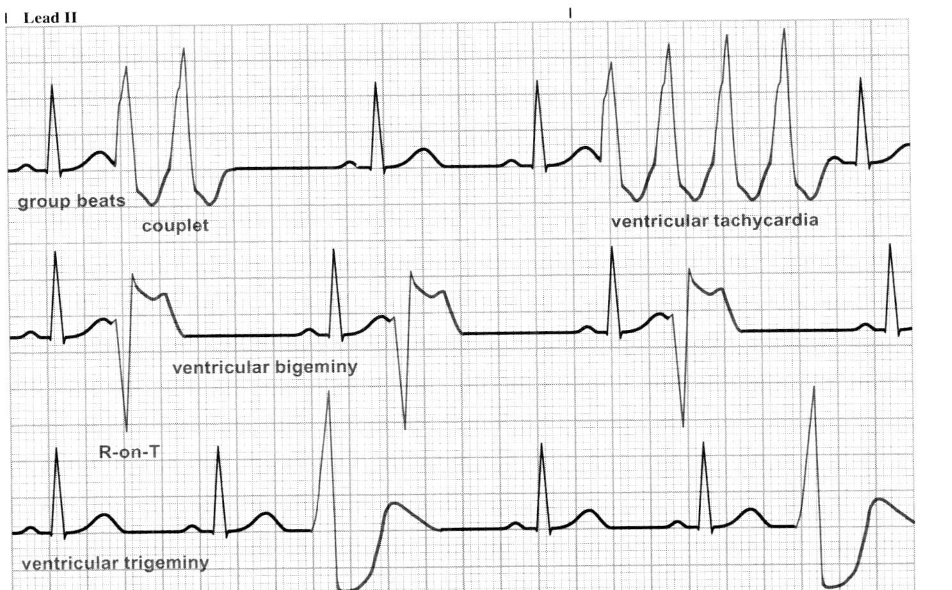

Ventricular Tachycardia (VT)

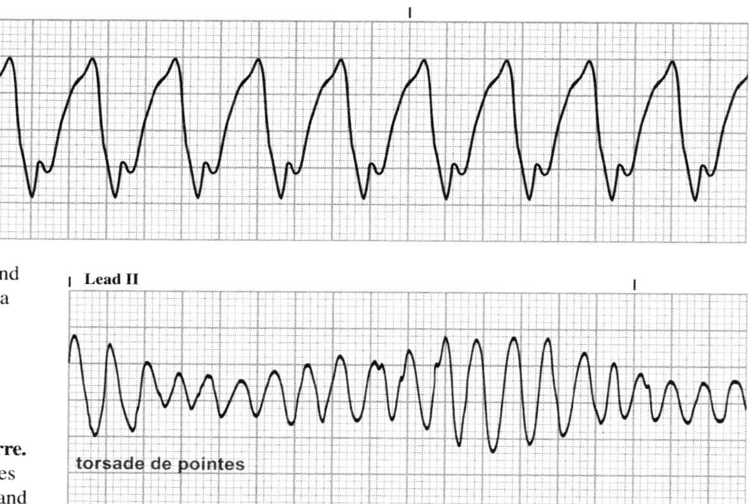

Heart Rate: Usually **110-250/min.**

Rhythm: Usually **regular,** but may be **slightly irregular.**

Pacemaker Site: An **ectopic pacemaker** in the **ventricles.**

P Waves: P waves may be present or absent. If present, they are usually of the underlying rhythm and bear no relation to the QRS complexes, sometimes appearing here and there as notches on the QRS complexes, ST segments and T waves. Uncommonly, negative P´waves related to the arrhythmia regularly follow the QRS complexes.

RP´ Intervals: Present if P´waves regularly follow the QRS complexes; **about 0.20 second or less.**

R-R Intervals: Usually **equal,** but may be **slightly unequal.**

QRS Complexes: Typically, **wide (0.12 sec or greater) and bizarre.** Usually identical but may vary slightly. When the QRS complexes vary greatly, gradually changing back and forth from one shape and direction to another over a series of beats, the ventricular tachycardia is called **torsade de pointes.**

Treatment: See pages 36, 38, and 39, Section II.

Ventricular Fibrillation (VF)

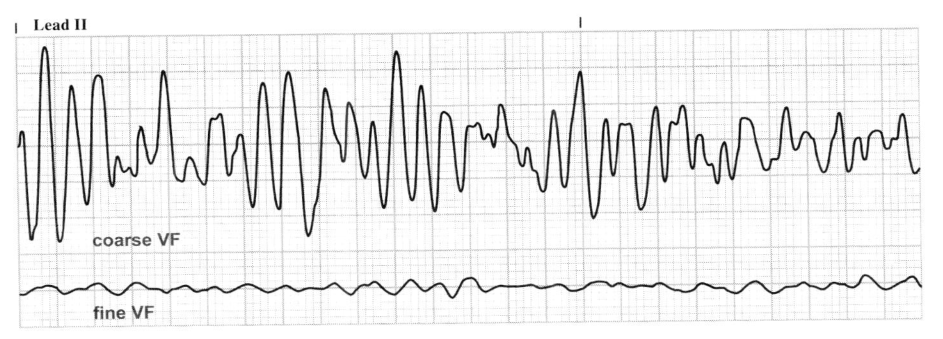

Heart Rate: 300-500/min.

Rhythm: Grossly (totally) irregular.

Pacemaker Site: Multiple **ectopic pacemakers** in the **ventricles.**

P Waves: None.

PR Intervals: None.

R-R Intervals: None.

QRS Complexes: Irregularly shaped, rounded (or pointed), and dissimilar **fibrillation (f) waves.** If the f waves are large **(>3 mm), "coarse" ventricular fibrillation** is present; if the f waves are small **(<3 mm), "fine" ventricular fibrillation** is present.

Treatment: See page 39, Section II.

First-degree AV Block

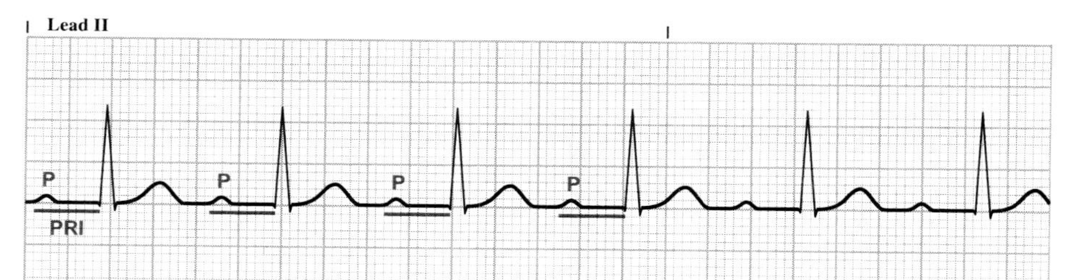

Heart Rate: The **atrial** and **ventricular rates** are typically the same.

Rhythm: That of the underlying rhythm.

P Waves: Those of the underlying rhythm; usually a QRS complex follows each P wave.

PR Intervals: Abnormal (greater than 0.20 sec); usually do not vary from beat to beat.

R-R Intervals: Those of the underlying rhythm.

QRS Complexes: Usually **normal (0.10 sec or less),** unless a preexisting intraventricular conduction disturbance is present.

AV Conduction Ratio: The AV conduction ratio is **1:1.**

Treatment: No specific treatment indicated.

Second-degree AV Block

Type I AV Block (Wenckebach)

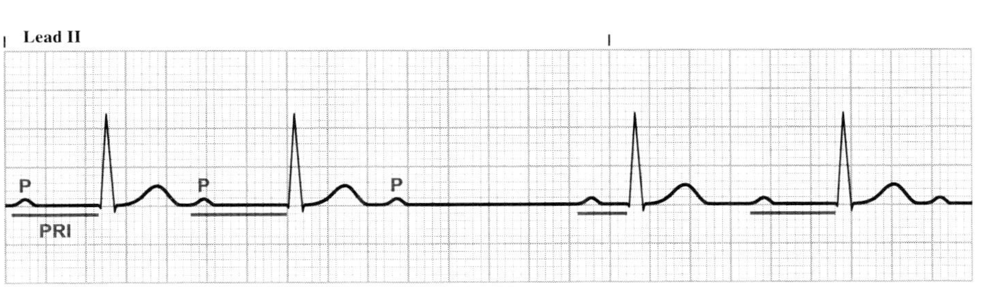

Heart Rate: The **atrial rate** is that of the underlying rhythm. The **ventricular rate** is typically less than the atrial rate.

Rhythm: The **atrial rhythm** is essentially **regular;** the **ventricular rhythm** is usually **irregular.**

P Waves: Those of the underlying rhythm; periodically a QRS complex fails to occur after a P wave (**nonconducted P wave** or **dropped beat**).

PR Intervals: Gradually lengthen until a **dropped beat** occurs, following which, the sequence begins anew.

R-R Intervals: **Unequal;** gradually **decrease** as the PR intervals lengthen until a **dropped beat** occurs, resulting in a **prolonged R-R interval.** Following this, the cycle begins anew.

QRS Complexes: Usually **normal (0.10 sec or less),** unless a preexisting intraventricular conduction disturbance is present.

AV Conduction Ratio: Commonly, the AV conduction ratio is **5:4, 4:3,** or **3:2** but may be **6:5. 7:6,** and so forth.

Treatment: See page 30, Section II.

Second-degree AV Block
Type II AV Block

Lead II

P P PRI P P P

Heart Rate: The **atrial rate** is that of the underlying rhythm. The **ventricular rate** is typically less than the atrial rate.

Rhythm: The **atrial rhythm** is essentially **regular;** the **ventricular rhythm** is usually **irregular.**

P Waves: Those of the underlying rhythm; periodically a QRS complex fails to occur after a P wave (**nonconducted P wave** or **dropped beat**).

PR Intervals: May be **normal (0.12-0.20 sec)** or **abnormal (greater than 0.20 sec);** usually **constant.**

R-R Intervals: Unequal.

QRS Complexes: Typically, **abnormal (greater than 0.12 sec)** because of a bundle branch block; rarely, **normal (0.10 sec or less).**

AV Conduction Ratio: The AV conduction ratio is commonly **4:3,** or **3:2** but may be **5:4. 6:5, 7:6,** and so forth.

Treatment: See page 30, Section II.

Second-degree AV Block

2:1 and High-degree (Advanced) AV Block

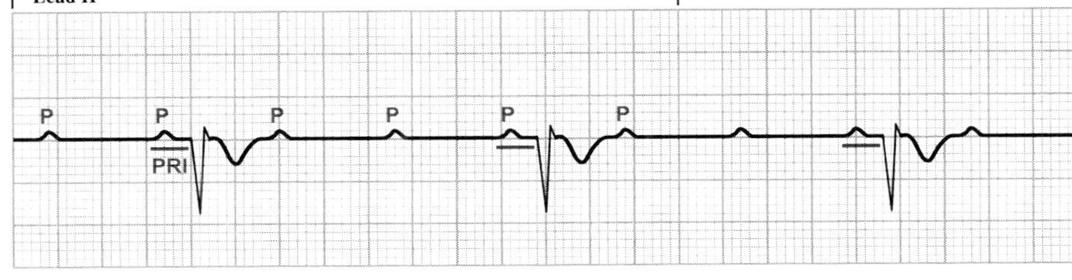

Heart Rate: The **atrial rate** is that of the underlying rhythm. The **ventricular rate** is typically less than the atrial rate.

Rhythm: The **atrial rhythm** is essentially **regular;** the **ventricular rhythm** may be **regular** or **irregular.**

P Waves: Those of the underlying rhythm; periodically, QRS complexes fail to occur after one or more P waves (**nonconducted P waves** or **dropped beats**).

PR Intervals: **Normal (0.12-0.20 sec)** or **abnormal (greater than 0.20 sec);** usually **constant.**

R-R Intervals: **Equal** or may **vary.**

QRS Complexes: **Normal (0.10 sec or less)** or **abnormal (greater than 0.12 sec)** because of a bundle branch block.

AV Conduction Ratio: Commonly, the AV conduction ratios are even numbers, **2:1, 4:1, 6:1, 8:1,** and so forth, but may be uneven numbers, **3:1** or **5:1.** A 3:1 or higher AV block is called a **high-degree (or advanced) AV block.**

Treatment: See page 31, Section II.

Third-degree AV Block

Lead II

Heart Rate: The **atrial rate** is that of the underlying rhythm. The **ventricular rate** is typically **40-60/min,** but may be **30-40/min or less** and independent of the atrial rate, i.e., **atrioventricular (AV) dissociation.**

Rhythm: The **atrial rhythm** is that of the underlying rhythm: **regular** or **irregular.** The **ventricular rhythm** is essentially **regular.**

Pacemaker Site: The **pacemaker site** of the P wave is the **SA node** or an **ectopic pacemaker** in the **atria** or **AV junction.** That of the QRS complex, an **escape pacemaker** in the **AV junction (junctional escape rhythm)** or **ventricles (ventricular escape rhythm).**

P Waves: The P waves occur independently of the QRS complexes.

PR Intervals: None.

R-R Intervals: Usually **equal.**

QRS Complexes: May be **normal (0.10 sec or less)** or **abnormal (greater than 0.12 sec).**

Treatment: See page 31, Section II.

Section II

Arrhythmia Management

Sinus Bradycardia
Sinus Arrest and Sinoatrial (SA) Exit Block
Second-degree, Type I AV Block (Wenckebach)

A. Asymptomatic

- **None.**

B. Symptomatic[1]

- Administer an **atropine 0.5- to 1.0-mg, rapid IV push.** Repeat every 3 to 5 min until the heart rate is **60 to 100/min** or the maximum dose of **2 to 3 mg (0.03 to 0.04 mg/kg)** of atropine has been administered.

  AND/OR

  Initiate **transcutaneous pacing.** (Administer **diazepam 5 to 15 mg** or **morphine 2 to 5 mg IV slowly** as needed for discomfort if the patient is conscious and not hypotensive.)
- Prepare for **immediate transvenous pacing.**

If symptomatic bradycardia and/or hypotension persist, increase the heart rate to **60 to 100/min** and the systolic blood pressure to **90 to 100 mm Hg** by administering:

- A **dopamine hydrochloride infusion** at a rate of **5 to 20 μg/kg/min.**

  OR

  An **epinephrine infusion** at a rate of **2 to 10 μg/min.**

Second-degree, Type II AV Block

A. Asymptomatic, in the presence of acute anteroseptal MI

- Attach a **transcutaneous pacemaker,** and put on **standby.**

B. Symptomatic

- Initiate **transcutaneous pacing.** (Administer **diazepam 5 to 15 mg** or **morphine 2 to 5 mg IV slowly** as needed for discomfort if the patient is conscious and not hypotensive.)
- Prepare for **immediate transvenous pacing.**

If symptomatic bradycardia and/or hypotension persist, increase the heart rate to **60 to 100/min** and the systolic blood pressure to **90 to 100 mm Hg** by administering:

- A **dopamine infusion** at a rate of **5 to 20 μg/kg/min.**

  OR

  An **epinephrine infusion** at a rate of **2 to 10 μg/min.**

[1]A bradycardia is considered **"symptomatic"** when one or more of the following clinical conditions or signs or symptoms are present:
- **Hypotension** or **shock** (systolic blood pressure, 80 to 90 mm Hg or less)
- **Congestive heart failure, pulmonary congestion**
- **Chest pain** or **dyspnea**
- **Decreased level of consciousness** caused by decreased cardiac output
- **PVCs,** particularly in the setting of an acute MI

Second-degree, 2:1 and High-degree (Advanced) AV Block
Third-degree AV Block

WITH NARROW QRS COMPLEXES

A. Asymptomatic

- **None.**

B. Symptomatic

- Administer an **atropine 0.5- to 1.0-mg, rapid IV push.** Repeat every 3 to 5 min until the heart rate is **60 to 100/min** or the maximum dose of **2 to 3 mg (0.03 to 0.04 mg/kg)** of atropine has been administered.

  AND/OR

  Initiate **transcutaneous pacing.** (Administer **diazepam 5 to 15 mg** or **morphine 2 to 5 mg IV slowly** as needed for discomfort if the patient is conscious and not hypotensive.)
- Prepare for **immediate transvenous pacing.**

If symptomatic bradycardia and/or hypotension persist, increase the heart rate to **60 to 100/min** and the systolic blood pressure to **90 to 100 mm Hg** by administering:

- A **dopamine infusion** at a rate of **5 to 20 μg/kg/min.**

  OR

  An **epinephrine infusion** at a rate of **2 to 10 μg/min.**

WITH WIDE QRS COMPLEXES

A. Asymptomatic, in the presence of acute anteroseptal MI

- Attach a **transcutaneous pacemaker,** and put on **standby.**

B. Symptomatic

- Initiate **transcutaneous pacing.** (Administer **diazepam 5 to 15 mg** or **morphine 2 to 5 mg IV slowly** as needed for discomfort if the patient is conscious and not hypotensive.)
- Prepare for **immediate transvenous pacing.**

If symptomatic bradycardia and/or hypotension persist, increase the heart rate to **60 to 100/min** and the systolic blood pressure to **90 to 100 mm Hg** by administering:

- A **dopamine infusion** at a rate of **5 to 20 μg/kg/min.**

  OR

  An **epinephrine infusion** at a rate of **2 to 10 μg/min.**

Junctional Escape Rhythm
Ventricular Escape Rhythm

A. Asymptomatic

- **None.**

B. Symptomatic

- Initiate **transcutaneous pacing.** (Administer **diazepam 5 to 15 mg** or **morphine 2 to 5 mg IV slowly** as needed for discomfort if the patient is conscious and not hypotensive.)
- Prepare for **immediate transvenous pacing.**

If symptomatic bradycardia and/or hypotension persist, increase the heart rate to **60 to 100/min** and the systolic blood pressure to **90 to 100 mm Hg** by administering:

- A **dopamine infusion** at a rate of **5 to 20 μg/kg/min.**

OR

An **epinephrine infusion** at a rate of **2 to 10 μg/min.**

Premature Atrial Contractions (PACs)
Premature Junctional Contractions (PJCs)

- Discontinue **stimulants** and **sympathomimetic drugs.**
- Administer **quinidine sulfate 200 mg orally.**

Paroxysmal Supraventricular Tachycardia (PSVT) with Narrow QRS Complexes (Paroxysmal Atrial Tachycardia [PAT] , Paroxysmal Junctional Tachycardia [PJT])

A. Patient's condition stable

- Perform **vagal maneuvers.**
- Administer an **adenosine 6-mg, rapid IV push** followed by a **20-ml flush of IV fluid.** In 1 to 2 min, repeat **adenosine 12 mg rapidly** followed by an **IV flush,** and repeat **once** in 1 to 2 min, if needed.
- Administer a **calcium channel blocker:**
  - **Verapamil 2.5 to 5.0 mg IV slowly** over 2 min. In 15 to 30 min, repeat **verapamil 5 to 10 mg IV,** if needed and no adverse affects.

    OR

    Diltiazem 20 mg (0.25 mg/kg) IV slowly over 2 min. In 15 min, repeat **diltiazem 25 mg (0.35 mg/kg),** if needed and no adverse effects.
- Deliver up to three **synchronized countershocks (50 J, 100 J, 200 J)** if **digitalis overdose not suspected.** (Administer **diazepam 5 to 15 mg** or **morphine 2 to 5 mg IV slowly** before cardioversion if the patient is conscious.)
- Consider **transcutaneous overdrive pacing.** (Administer **diazepam 5 to 15 mg** or **morphine 2 to 5 mg IV slowly** as needed for discomfort if the patient is conscious and not hypotensive.)

B. Patient's condition unstable[2]

- Deliver up to three **synchronized countershocks (50 J, 100 J, 200 J)** if **digitalis overdose not suspected.** (Administer **diazepam 5 to 15 mg** or **morphine 2 to 5 mg IV slowly** before cardioversion if the patient is conscious.)
- Consider **transcutaneous overdrive pacing.** (Administer **diazepam 5 to 15 mg** or **morphine 2 to 5 mg IV slowly** as needed for discomfort if the patient is conscious and not hypotensive.)

[2]A patient's condition is considered **"unstable"** when one or more of the following clinical conditions or signs or symptoms are present:

- **Hypotension** or **shock** (systolic blood pressure, 80 to 90 mm Hg or less)
- **Congestive heart failure, pulmonary congestion**
- **Chest pain** or **dyspnea**
- **Decreased level of consciousness** caused by decreased cardiac output
- **Acute MI**

Atrial Flutter
Nonparoxysmal Atrial Tachycardia without Block

A. Heart rate over 150 beats/min and patient's condition stable

- Consider the administration of a **calcium channel blocker:**
  - **Diltiazem 20 mg (0.25 mg/kg) IV slowly** over 2 min. In 15 min, repeat **diltiazem 25 mg (0.35 mg/kg),** if needed and no adverse effects.

    OR

    Verapamil 2.5 to 5.0 mg IV slowly over 2 min. In 15 to 30 min, repeat **verapamil 5 to 10 mg IV,** if needed and no adverse affects.

    OR
- Consider the delivery of a **synchronized countershock (50 J).** (Administer **diazepam 5 to 15 mg** or **morphine 2 to 5 mg IV slowly** before cardioversion if the patient is conscious and not hypotensive.)
- Deliver a **synchronized countershock (50 J)** if a **calcium channel blocker** was administered initially.

  OR

  Repeat the **synchronized countershock** once or twice **(100 J, 200J)** or administer a **calcium channel blocker** as above, if cardioversion was attempted initially.

B. Heart rate over 150 beats/min and patient's condition unstable

- Deliver one or more **synchronized countershocks (50 J, 100 J, 200 J).** (Administer **diazepam 5 to 15 mg** or **morphine 2 to 5 mg IV slowly** before cardioversion if the patient is conscious and not hypotensive.)

Atrial Fibrillation

A. Patient's condition stable

- Consider the administration of a **calcium channel blocker:**
  - **Diltiazem 20 mg (0.25 mg/kg) IV slowly** over 2 min. In 15 min, repeat **diltiazem 25 mg (0.35 mg/kg),** if needed and no adverse effects.

    OR

    Verapamil 2.5 to 5.0 mg IV slowly over 2 min. In 15 to 30 min, repeat **verapamil 5 to 10 mg IV,** if needed and no adverse affects.

B. Patient's condition unstable and atrial fibrillation of recent origin and of short duration (less than 2 days)

- Administer one or more **synchronized countershocks (100 J, 200 J).** (Administer **diazepam 5 to 15 mg** or **morphine 2 to 5 mg IV slowly** before cardioversion if the patient is conscious and not hypotensive.)

  If atrial fibrillation has been present for 2 or more days, consider anticoagulation over a period of time before cardioversion.

Premature Ventricular Contractions (PVCs)

A. Patient's condition stable or unstable

If PVCs occur in a suspected acute MI or in an ischemic episode:

- Consider the administration of the following **antiarrhythmic agents:**
  - A **lidocaine 1.0- to 1.5-mg/kg IV bolus slowly,** and repeat a **lidocaine 0.5- to 0.75-mg/kg IV bolus slowly** every 5 to 10 min until the **PVCs** are suppressed or a total dose of **3 mg/kg of lidocaine** has been administered.

    If lidocaine suppresses the PVCs, start a **maintenance infusion of lidocaine** at a rate of **2 to 4 mg/min.**

  - A **procainamide hydrochloride infusion** at a rate of **20 to 30 mg/min** until (1) the **PVCs** are suppressed, (2) a total dose of 17 mg/kg of procainamide has been administered, (3) side effects from procainamide appear, or (4) the QRS complex widens by 50% of its original width.

    If procainamide suppresses the PVCs, start a **maintenance infusion of procainamide** at a rate of **1 to 4 mg/min.**

  - **Bretylium tosylate 5 to 10 mg/kg, diluted to 50 mL, IV slowly** over 8 to 10 min. Start a **maintenance infusion of bretylium** at a rate of **1 to 2 mg/min** up to a total dose of 30 mg/kg.
- Consider **transcutaneous overdrive pacing.** (Administer **diazepam 5 to 15 mg** or **morphine 2 to 5 mg IV slowly** as needed for discomfort if the patient is conscious and not hypotensive.)

Wide-QRS-Complex Tachycardia of Unknown Origin (with Pulse)

A. Patient's condition stable

- Administer a **lidocaine 1.0- to 1.5-mg/kg IV bolus slowly,** and repeat a **lidocaine 0.5- to 0.75-mg/kg IV bolus slowly** every 5 to 10 min until the **tachycardia** is suppressed or a total dose of **3 mg/kg of lidocaine** has been administered.

  If lidocaine suppresses the tachycardia, start a **maintenance infusion of lidocaine** at a rate of **2 to 4 mg/min.**
- Administer an **adenosine 6-mg, rapid IV push** followed by a **20-ml flush of IV fluid.** In 1 to 2 min, repeat **adenosine 12 mg rapidly** followed by an **IV flush,** and repeat **once** in 1 to 2 min, if needed.
- Consider **transcutaneous overdrive pacing.** (Administer **diazepam 5 to 15 mg** or **morphine 2 to 5 mg IV slowly** as needed for discomfort if the patient is conscious and not hypotensive.)

If the tachycardia persists and the patient's condition remains stable, refer to Ventricular Tachycardia (VT) (with Pulse), A. Patient's condition stable on **page 36,** and administer **procainamide** and **bretylium** and deliver **synchronized countershocks** as indicated.

If the tachycardia persists and the patient's condition becomes unstable, refer to Ventricular Tachycardia (VT) (with Pulse), B. Patient's condition unstable on **page 37,** and deliver **unsynchronized shocks** and administer **procainamide** and **bretylium,** and so forth, as indicated.

Ventricular Tachycardia (VT) (with Pulse)

A. Patient's condition stable

- Administer a **lidocaine 1.0- to 1.5-mg/kg IV bolus slowly,** and repeat a **lidocaine 0.5- to 0.75-mg/kg IV bolus slowly** every 5 to 10 min until the **VT** is terminated or a total dose of **3 mg/kg of lidocaine** has been administered.

  If lidocaine converts the VT, start a **maintenance infusion of lidocaine** at a rate of **2 to 4 mg/min.**

- Administer a **procainamide infusion** at a rate of **20 to 30 mg/min** until (1) the **VT** is terminated, (2) a total dose of 17 mg/kg of procainamide has been administered, (3) side effects from procainamide appear, or (4) the QRS complex widens by 50% of its original width.

  If procainamide converts the VT, start a **maintenance infusion of procainamide** at a rate of **1 to 4 mg/min.**

- Administer **bretylium 5 to 10 mg/kg, diluted to 50 mL, IV slowly** over 8 to 10 min. Start a **maintenance infusion of bretylium** at a rate of **1 to 2 mg/min** up to a total dose of 30 mg/kg.
- Deliver **one or more synchronized countershocks** at increasing energy levels (100 J, 200 J, 300 J, 360 J). (Administer **diazepam 5 to 15 mg** or **morphine 2 to 5 mg IV slowly** before cardioversion if the patient is conscious and not hypotensive.)

If the ventricular tachycardia persists or recurs and the patient's condition becomes unstable:

- Deliver one or more **unsynchronized shocks** (beginning at 100 J or the energy level last used and increasing at progressively higher energy levels as needed). (Administer **diazepam 5 to 15 mg** or **morphine 2 to 5 mg IV slowly** before cardioversion if the patient is conscious and not hypotensive.)
- Consider **transcutaneous overdrive pacing.** (Administer **diazepam 5 to 15 mg** or **morphine 2 to 5 mg IV slowly** as needed for discomfort if the patient is conscious and not hypotensive.)

If the ventricular tachycardia persists:

- Continue administrating the **antiarrhythmic agents** listed on the left, and repeat the **unsynchronized shocks** as above.

If shocks are effective in terminating the ventricular tachycardia:

- Continue or start a **maintenance infusion of the arrhythmic drug** that was being administered at the time of termination of the **VT** or administer the next **arrhythmic drug** listed on the left.

Ventricular Tachycardia (VT) (with Pulse) (Cont.)

B. Patient's condition unstable

- Deliver up to three **unsynchronized shocks (100 J, 200 J, 300 J, 360 J).** (Administer **diazepam 5 to 15 mg** or **morphine 2 to 5 mg IV slowly** before cardioversion if the patient is conscious and not hypotensive.)

If shocks are effective in terminating the ventricular tachycardia:

- Administer a **lidocaine 1.0- to 1.5-mg/kg IV bolus slowly**, and start a **maintenance infusion of lidocaine** at a rate of **2 to 4 mg/min.**

If shocks are not effective in terminating the ventricular tachycardia:

- Administer a **lidocaine 1.0- to 1.5-mg/kg IV bolus slowly,** and repeat a **lidocaine 0.5- to 0.75-mg/kg IV bolus slowly** every 5 to 10 min until the **VT** is terminated or a total dose of **3 mg/kg of lidocaine** has been administered.

  If lidocaine terminates the VT, start a **maintenance infusion of lidocaine** at a rate of **2 to 4 mg/min.**

- Deliver an **unsynchronized shock (at energy level last used),** and repeat the **unsynchronized shocks** at progressively increasing energy levels as needed.
- Administer a **procainamide infusion** at a rate of **20 to 30 mg/min** until (1) the **VT** is terminated, (2) a total dose of 17 mg/kg of procainamide has been administered, (3) side effects from procainamide appear, or (4) the QRS complex widens by 50% of its original width.

  If procainamide terminates the VT, start a **maintenance infusion of procainamide** at a rate of **1 to 4 mg/min.**

- Deliver an **unsynchronized shock** (at the energy level last used), and repeat the **unsynchronized shock** at progressively increasing energy levels as needed.
- Administer **bretylium 5 to 10 mg/kg, diluted to 50 mL, IV slowly** over 8 to 10 min. Start a **maintenance infusion of bretylium** at a rate of **1 to 2 mg/min** up to a total dose of 30 mg/kg.
- Consider **transcutaneous overdrive pacing.**

If the ventricular tachycardia recurs at any time following successful termination:

- Deliver an **unsynchronized shock** (at the energy level last used), and repeat the **unsynchronized shock** at progressively increasing energy levels as needed.

Torsade de Pointes (with Pulse)

A. Patient's condition stable or unstable

- Perform **transcutaneous overdrive pacing.** (Administer **diazepam 5 to 15 mg** or **morphine 2 to 5 mg IV slowly** as needed for discomfort if the patient is conscious and not hypotensive.)
- Administer **magnesium 1 to 2 g, diluted to 10 mL, intravenously** over 1 to 2 min if the patient is not hypotensive. Start a **maintenance infusion of magnesium 1 to 2 g, diluted to 100 mL,** to run over 1 hr.
- Deliver up to three **unsynchronized shocks (200 J, 300 J, 360 J).** (Administer **diazepam 5 to 15 mg** or **morphine 2 to 5 mg IV slowly** before delivering the first shock, if not administered previously and if the patient is conscious and not hypotensive.)

Ventricular Fibrillation/Pulseless Ventricular Tachycardia (VF/VT)

A. Unmonitored cardiac arrest

- Perform **CPR.**
- **Defibrillate** up to three times **(200 J, 300 J, 360 J).**
- Continue **CPR** for the duration of the resuscitation.
- **Intubate,** and **establish an IV line.**
- Administer an **epinephrine 1-mg IV push** followed by a **20-mL flush of IV fluid,** and repeat every 3 to 5 min during resuscitation. (**If no IV line,** administer **epinephrine 2.0 to 2.5 mg via an ET tube,** and repeat if needed.)
- **Defibrillate (360 J)** 30 to 60 sec after each epinephrine dose.

If VF/VT is terminated at any time above:

- Administer a **lidocaine 1.0- to 1.5-mg/kg IV bolus slowly**, and start a **maintenance infusion of lidocaine** at a rate of **2 to 4 mg/min.**

If VF/VT persists, administer the following **antiarrhythmic agents,** and **defibrillate (360 J)** 30 to 60 sec after each drug dose:

- A **lidocaine 1.0- to 1.5-mg/kg IV push** followed by a **20-mL flush of IV fluid.** Repeat **once** in 3 to 5 min up to a total dose of 3 mg/kg. (**If no IV line,** administer **lidocaine 2 to 3 mg/kg via an ET tube,** and repeat if needed.) **If VT/VF is terminated,** start a **maintenance infusion of lidocaine** at a rate of **2 to 4 mg/min.**
- A **bretylium 5-mg/kg IV push** followed by a **20-mL flush of IV fluid.** In 5 min, administer a **bretylium 10-mg/kg IV push** and a **20-mL flush of IV fluid,** and repeat **once or twice** up to a total dose of 30 mg/kg. **If VT/VF is terminated,** start a **maintenance infusion of bretylium** at a rate of **1 to 2 mg/min.**

(Continued on next page.)

Ventricular Fibrillation/Pulseless Ventricular Tachycardia (VF/VT) (Cont.)

- A **procainamide infusion** at a rate of **30 mg/min** up to a total dose of 17 mg/kg. **If VT/VF is terminated,** start a **maintenance infusion of procainamide** at a rate of **1 to 2 mg/min.**
- Consider a **magnesium 1- to 2-g IV push** followed by a **20-mL flush of IV fluid** if torsade de pointes or a hypomagnesic state is present.
- Consider a **sodium bicarbonate 1-mEq/kg IV b1olus** if indicated[3].

Any time VT/VF is terminated:

- Continue **CPR** until the patient's pulse is palpable and the systolic blood pressure is **90 to 100 mm Hg** or greater.

If a symptomatic bradycardia or tachycardia occurs, consider treating the arrhythmia using the appropriate **treatment protocol.**

If hypotension is present (systolic blood pressure, 80 to 90 mm Hg or less) in the absence of pulmonary edema.

- Consider **fluid boluses of 250 to 500 mL of 0.9% saline or Ringer's lactate solution** while monitoring the vital signs and the lungs for edema.

If the systolic blood pressure is <70 mm Hg:

- Start a **norepinephrine infusion** at an initial rate of **0.5 to 1 μg/min,** and then infuse up to **8 to 30 μg/min** to increase the systolic blood pressure to **70 to 100 mm Hg,** and then switch to **dopamine.**

OR

If the systolic blood pressure is >70 mm Hg:

- Start a **dopamine infusion** at an initial rate of **2.5 μg/kg/min,** and then infuse up to **20 μg/kg/min** to increase the systolic blood pressure to **90 to 100 mm Hg.**

If severe pulmonary edema is present and the patient is not hypotensive (i.e, the systolic blood pressure is greater than 100 mm Hg):

- Place the patient in a **semireclining or full upright position with the legs dependent,** if possible.
- Administer **two 0.4-mg nitroglycerin tablets sublingually,** and repeat twice every 5 to 10 min if needed.

AND/OR

- Administer **morphine 1 to 3 mg IV slowly,** and repeat in 5 min if needed.
- Administer **furosemide 20 to 40 mg IV slowly** over 1 to 2 min.

If VT/VF recurs:

- **Defibrillate,** beginning at an energy level last effective at defibrillation, perform **CPR,** and administer **epinephrine, lidocaine, bretylium, procainamide,** and **magnesium** within their dose limits as before.

B. Monitored cardiac arrest

- Consider a **precordial thump.**
- **Defibrillate** up to three times **(200 J, 300 J, 360 J).**
- Perform **CPR.**
- **Intubate,** and **establish an IV line.**
- Administer **epinephrine, defibrillate,** administer **lidocaine, bretylium, procainamide,** and **magnesium,** and so forth, as in **A. Unmonitored cardiac arrest** on **page 38**.

[3]Indications for bicarbonate are **preexisting metabolic acidosis, hyperkalemia,** or **tricyclic** or **phenobarbital overdose.**

Pulseless Electrical Activity (PEA)

A. Unmonitored cardiac arrest

- Perform **CPR, intubate,** and **establish an IV line.**
- Administer an **epinephrine 1-mg IV push** followed by a **20-mL flush of IV fluid,** and repeat every 3 to 5 min during resuscitation. (**If no IV line,** administer **epinephrine 2.0 to 2.5 mg via an ET tube,** and repeat if needed.)
- Consider a **sodium bicarbonate 1-mEq/kg IV bolus** if indicated.
- Continue **CPR** for the duration of the resuscitation.
- Treat any **underlying condition.**

If the heart rate is 80 per min or less:

- Administer an **atropine 1-mg, rapid IV push followed by a 20-mL flush of IV fluid.** Repeat every 3 to 5 min until the maximum dose of **3.0 mg (0.04 mg/kg)** of atropine has been administered. (**If no IV line,** administer **atropine 1 to 2 mg, diluted up to 10 mL, via an ET tube,** and repeat if needed.)

If hypovolemia is suspected:

- Consider **fluid boluses of 250 to 500 mL of 0.9% saline or Ringer's lactate solution** while monitoring the patient's pulse.

B. Monitored cardiac arrest

- Consider **transcutaneous pacing.**
- Perform **CPR.**
- **Intubate,** and **establish an IV line.**
- Administer **epinephrine,** continue **CPR,** administer **atropine,** and so forth, as in **A. Unmonitored cardiac arrest** on the left.

Ventricular Asystole

A. Unmonitored cardiac arrest

- Perform **CPR, intubate,** and **establish an IV line.**
- Consider **immediate transcutaneous pacing** if cardiac arrest is witnessed or of known short duration.
- Continue **CPR** for the duration of the resuscitation.
- Administer an **epinephrine 1-mg IV push** followed by a **20-mL flush of IV fluid,** and repeat every 3 to 5 min during resuscitation. (**If no IV line,** administer **epinephrine 2.0 to 2.5 mg via an ET tube,** and repeat if needed.)
- Administer an **atropine 1-mg, rapid IV push followed by a 20-mL flush of IV fluid.** Repeat every 3 to 5 min until the maximum dose of **3.0 mg (0.04 mg/kg)** of atropine has been administered. (**If no IV line,** administer **atropine 1 to 2 mg, diluted up to 10 mL, via an ET tube,** and repeat if needed.)
- Consider a **sodium bicarbonate 1-mEq/kg IV bolus** if indicated.

If ventricular asystole persists:

- Repeat **epinephrine** and **atropine,** and continue **CPR.**

B. Monitored cardiac arrest

- Consider **immediate transcutaneous pacing.**
- Perform **CPR.**
- **Intubate,** and **establish an IV line.**
- Administer **epinephrine,** continue **CPR,** administer **atropine,** and so forth, as in **A. Unmonitored cardiac arrest** on the left.

Section III

Bundle Branch and Fascicular Blocks

Right Bundle Branch Block (RBBB)

QRS Duration: **≥0.12 second** in **complete RBBB; 0.10 to 0.11 second** in **incomplete RBBB.**

QRS Axis: **Normal** or **right axis deviation** (**+90°** to **+110°**).

ST Segments: May be **depressed** in leads V_1-V_3.

T Waves: May be **inverted** in leads V_1-V_3.

QRS Complexes:

With an intact interventricular septum

Lead V_1 and V_2

Wide QRS with a classic **triphasic rSR´** (**"M"** or **"rabbit ears"**) pattern:

- **Initial small r wave**
- **Deep, slurred S wave**
- **Late (terminal) tall R´ wave**

Leads I, aVL, and V_5-V_6

Wide QRS with a typical **qRS** pattern:

- **Initial small q wave**
- **Tall R wave**
- **Late (terminal) deep, slurred S wave**

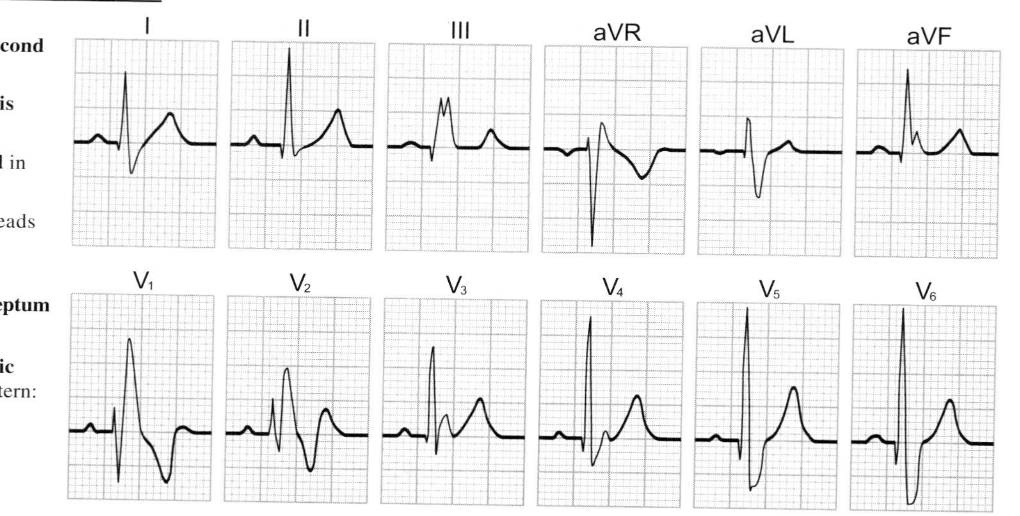

QRS Complexes:

Without an intact interventricular septum

Lead V_1 and V_2

Wide QRS with a **QSR** pattern:

- **Absent initial small r wave**
- **Deep QS wave**
- **Late (terminal) tall R wave**

Leads I, aVL, and V_5-V_6

Wide QRS with an **RS** pattern:

- **Absent initial small q wave**
- **Tall R wave**
- **Late (terminal) deep, slurred S wave**

Left Bundle Branch Block (LBBB)

QRS Duration: **≥0.12 second** in **complete LBBB; 0.10 to 0.11 second** in **incomplete LBBB.**

QRS Axis: Commonly, **left axis deviation** (**-30°** to **-90°**), but may be **normal.**

ST Segments: **Depressed** in leads I, aVL, and V_5-V_6; **elevated** in leads V_1-V_3.

T Waves: **Inverted** in leads I, aVL, V_5-V_6; **elevated** in leads V_1-V_3.

QRS Complexes:

With an intact interventricular septum

Lead V_1-V_3

Wide QRS with an **rS** or **QS** pattern:

- **Initial small r wave**
- **Deep, wide S wave**

OR

- **Absent R wave**
- **Deep, wide QS wave**

Leads I, aVL, and V_5-V_6

Wide QRS with an **R** or **rsR´** pattern:

- **Absent initial small q wave**
- **Tall, wide, slurred R wave with or without notching and/or an rsR´ pattern,** and with a **prolonged VAT**

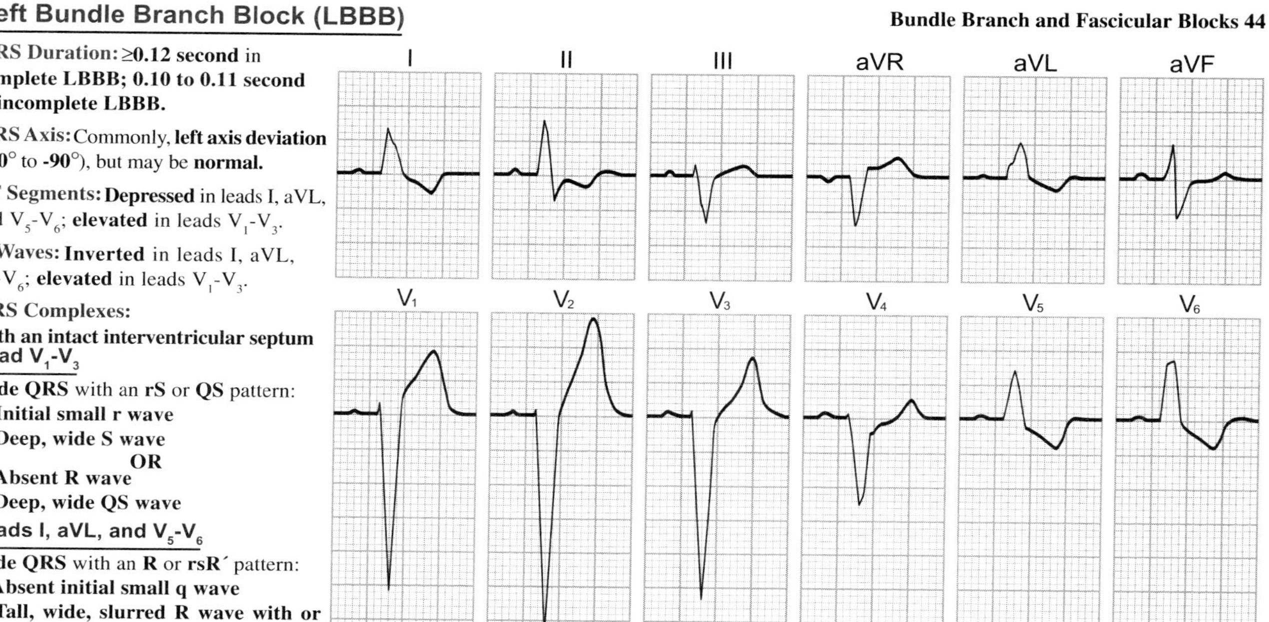

QRS Complexes:

Without an intact interventricular septum

Leads V_1 and V_2

Wide QRS with an **rS** pattern:

- **Small narrow r wave**
- **Deep, wide S wave**

Leads I, aVL, and V_5-V_6

Wide QRS with a **qR** pattern:

- **Small q wave**
- **Tall, wide, slurred R wave with or without notching and/or an rsR´ pattern,** and with a **prolonged VAT**

I

aVL

V_1

V_2

V_5

V_6

Left Anterior Fascicular Block (LAFB)

QRS Duration: **Normal, <0.10 second.**

QRS Axis: **Left axis deviation (-30° to -90°).**

ST Segments: **Normal.**

T Waves: **Normal.**

QRS Complexes:

Leads I and aVL

Narrow QRS:

- **Initial small q wave**

Leads II, III, and aVF

Narrow QRS:

- **Initial small r wave**
- **Deep S wave,** typically larger than the **R wave**

QRS Pattern: A typical **q_1r_3 pattern** is present.

Left Posterior Fascicular Block (LPFB)

QRS Duration: **Normal, <0.10 second.**

QRS Axis: **Right axis deviation ($+110^\circ$ to $+180^\circ$).**

ST Segments: **Normal.**

T Waves: **Normal.**

QRS Complexes:

Leads I, aVL, and V_5-V_6

Narrow QRS:

- **Initial small r wave** in **leads I and aVL**
- **Deep S wave** in **leads I and aVL**

Leads II, III, and aVF

Narrow QRS:

- **Initial small q wave**
- **Tall R wave**

QRS Pattern: A typical **q_3r_1 pattern** is present.

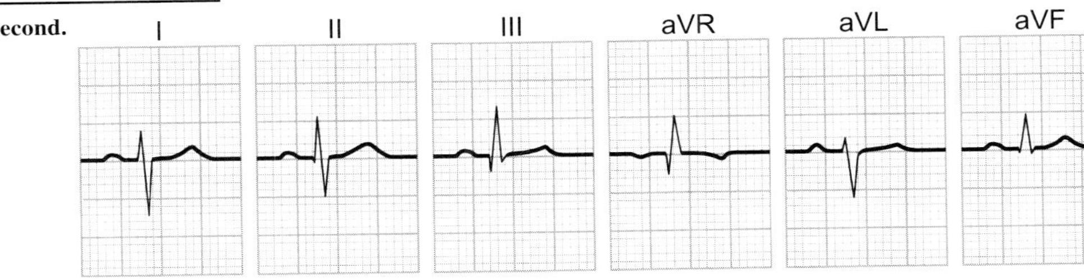

Section IV

Miscellaneous ECG Changes

Chamber Enlargement
Pericarditis
Electrolyte Imbalance
Drug Effect
Pulmonary Disease

Right Ventricular Hypertrophy (RVH)

P Waves: **Right atrial enlargement** usually present.

QRS Complexes:

Duration: 0.10 second or less.

Ventricular Activation Time (VAT): Prolonged beyond the upper normal limit of 0.03 second in leads V_1-V_2.

Q Waves: May be present in leads II, III, and aVF.

R Waves: **Tall R waves** in leads II, III, and V_1. Usually 7 mm or more (≥0.7 mV) in height and equal to or greater than the S waves in depth in lead V_1. **Relatively tall R waves** also in leads V_2-V_3.

Note: Tall R waves equal to or greater than the S waves in lead V_1 may also be present in acute posterior myocardial infarction and in counterclockwise rotation of the heart.

S Waves: Relatively deeper than normal in leads I and V_4-V_6. In lead V_6, the depth of the S waves may be greater than the height of the R waves.

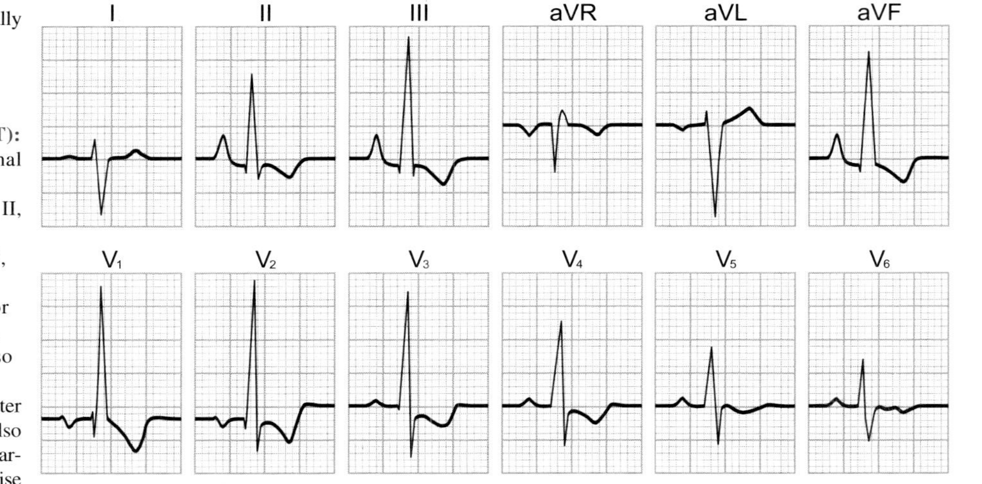

ST Segments: **"Downsloping" ST segment depression** of 1 mm or more may be present in leads II, III, aVF, and V_1 and sometimes in leads V_2 and V_3.

T Waves: Often **inverted** in leads II, III, aVF, and V_1 and sometimes in leads V_2 and V_3.

Note: The downsloping ST segment depression and the T wave inversion together form the **"strain" pattern** characteristic of longstanding RVH, giving the so-called **"hockey stick"** appearance to the QRS-ST-T complex.

QRS Axis: **Right axis deviation** of +90° or more; **≥+110°** in adults; **≥+120°** in the young.

Right Atrial Enlargement

P Waves:

Duration: Usually normal (0.10 second or less).
P Wave Shape: Typically **tall and symmetrically peaked P waves** in leads II, III, and aVF—the **P pulmonale**. **Sharply peaked biphasic P waves** in lead V_1.
Direction: **Positive (upright)** in leads II, III, and aVF; **biphasic** in V_1 with the initial deflection greater than the terminal deflection.
Amplitude: 2.5 mm or greater in leads II, III, and aVF.

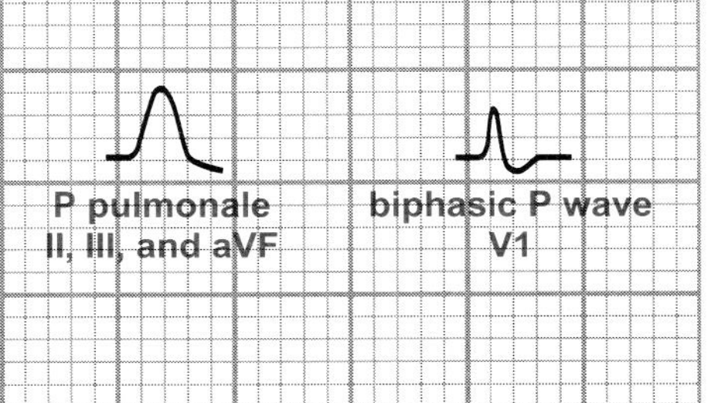

Left Ventricular Hypertrophy (LVH)

P Waves: **Left atrial enlargement** usually present.

QRS Complexes:

- **Duration:** Normal, 0.10 second or less.
- **Ventricular Activation Time (VAT):** Prolonged beyond the upper normal limit to **0.05 second or more** in leads V_5 and V_6.
- **R Waves:** **Tall R waves** in leads I, aVL, and V_5-V_6.
- **S Waves:** **Deep S waves** in leads III and V_1.

QRS Axis: Usually normal, but may be **left axis deviation (>-30°).**

ST Segments: **"Downsloping" ST segment depression** of 1 mm or more in leads I, aVL, and V_5-V_6.

T Waves: **Inverted** in leads I, aVL, and V_5-V_6. The **inverted T waves** together with the **"downsloping" ST segment depression** form the **"strain" pattern** characteristic of longstanding LVH—the so-called **"hockey stick"** appearance of the QRS-ST-T complex.

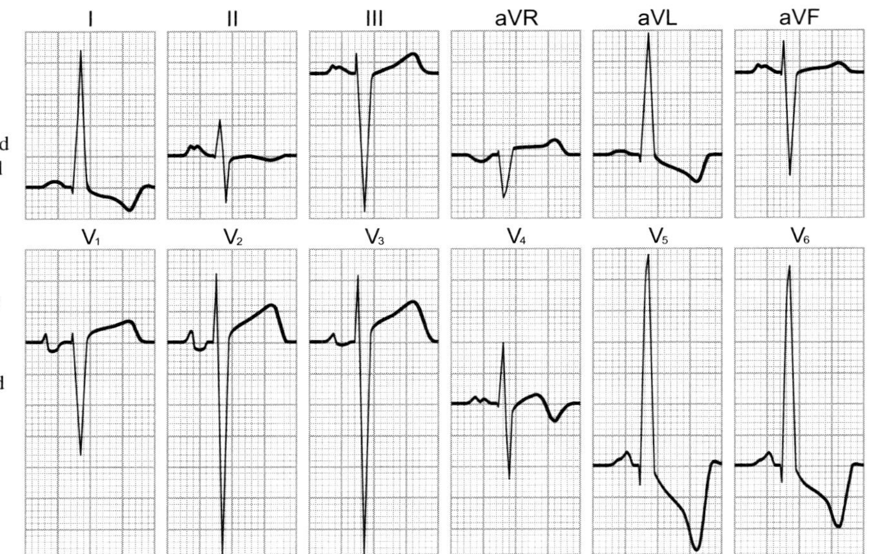

Diagnosis of LVH: The **amplitude (or voltage) of the R waves** and the **depth (or voltage) of the S waves** considered to indicate LVH in certain leads are shown in the following table.

	Lead				
Wave	**I**	**III**	**aVL**	**V_1 or V_2**	**V_5 or V_6**
R	≥20 mm (≥2.0 mV)		≥11 mm (≥1.1 mV)		≥30 mm (≥3.0 mV)
S		≥20 mm (≥2.0 mV)		≥30 mm (≥3.0 mV)	

Sum of R and S Waves: The sum of the amplitude of the R waves and the depth of the S waves (in mm or mV) in certain leads with the most prominent R and S waves is diagnostic of LVH if it equals or exceeds the following values:

R I + S III = ≥25 mm (≥2.5 mV)

S V_1 (or S V_2) + R V_5 (or R V_6) = ≥35 mm (≥3.5 mV)

Criteria Diagnostic of LVH

LVH is present if **criteria 1** and **2** are met:

Criteria 1: **R I OR S III = ≥20 mm (≥2.0 mV)**

OR

R I + S III = ≥25 mm (≥2.5 mV)

OR

S V_1 (or S V_2) + R V_5 (or R V_6) = ≥35 mm (≥3.5 mV)

Criteria 2: **QRS axis between -15° and -30° or greater than -30° (left axis deviation),**

OR

ST segment depression of ≥1 mm in leads with an R wave having the amplitude (or voltage) criteria of left ventricular hypertrophy. (See the table to the left.)

Left Atrial Enlargement

P Waves:

Duration: Usually greater than 0.10 second.

P Wave Shape: A **broad positive (upright) P wave,** 0.12 second or greater in duration, in any lead. A **wide, notched P wave** with two "humps" 0.04 second or more apart—the **P mitrale,** usually present in leads I, II, and V_4-V_6. The first hump represents the depolarization of the right atrium, the second hump, the enlarged left atrium. A **biphasic P wave,** greater than 0.10 second in total duration, with the terminal, negative component 1 mm (0.1 mV) or more deep and 1 mm (0.04 second) or more in duration, i.e., **1 small square** or **greater,** commonly present in leads V_1-V_2. The initial, positive (upright) component of the P wave represents the depolarization of the right atrium; the terminal, negative component, the depolarization of the enlarged left atrium.

Direction: **Positive (upright)** in leads I, II, and V_4-V_6 and biphasic in leads V_1-V_2; may be **negative** in leads III and aVF.

Amplitude: Usually normal (0.5 to 2.5 mm).

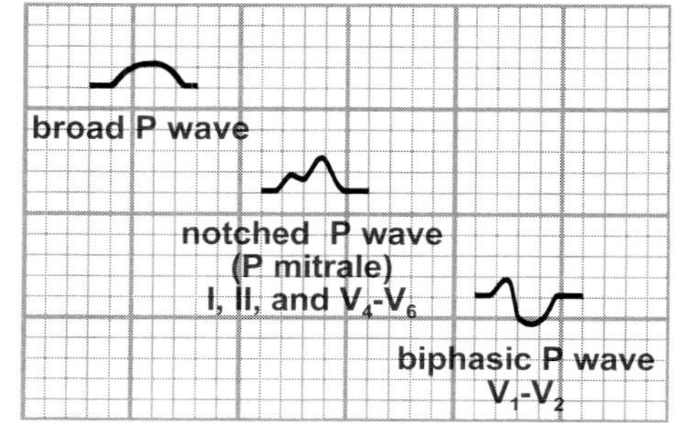

Pericarditis

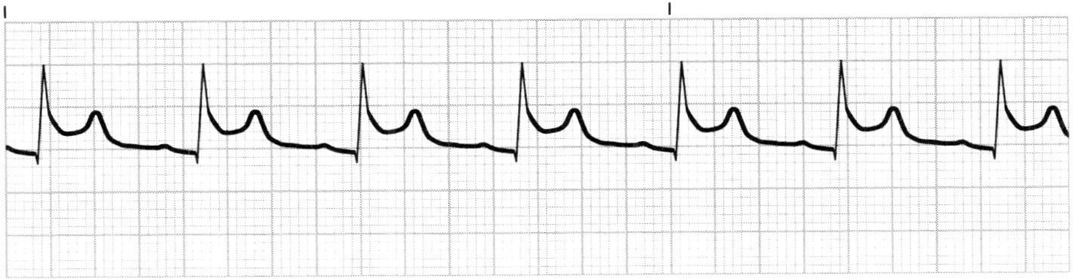

QRS Complexes:

Amplitude: **Normal** if **pleural effusion** absent. QRS complexes may be low in voltage (amplitude) if pleural effusion is present. If pleural effusion is severe, **cardiac tamponade** may occur, causing the QRS complexes to alternate between normal and low voltage, coincident with respiration **(electrical alternans).**

Abnormal Q waves/QS complexes: Absent.

ST Segments: **Elevated (concave elevation)** in acute phase of pericarditis in the ECG leads overlying the affected pericardium. (See table at right.) **Reciprocal ST segment depression** except in lead aVR is usually not present. The ST segments return to **normal** as the pericarditis resolves.

Location of Pericarditis	Leads with ST Segment Elevation
Anterior	I, V_2-V_4
Lateral	I, aVL, V_5-V_6
Inferior	II, III, aVL
Generalized	I, II, III, aVL, aVF, V_2-V_6

T Waves: **Elevated** during the acute phase of pericarditis in the leads with ST segment elevation. The elevated T waves become **inverted** as the pericarditis resolves.

QT Intervals: Normal.

Hyperkalemia

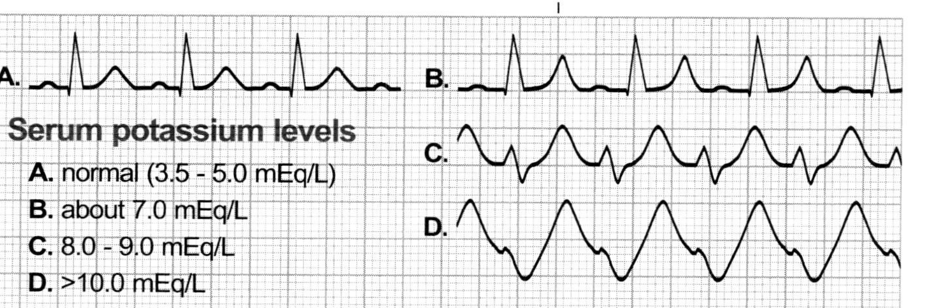

P Waves: Begin to flatten out and become wider at a serum potassium level of about 6.5 mEq/L; and disappear at levels of about 7.0-9.0 mEq/L.

PR Intervals: May be **normal** or **prolonged,** greater than 0.20 second. Absent when the P waves disappear.

QRS Complexes: Begin to widen at serum potassium levels of about 6.0-6.5 mEq/L, becoming markedly slurred and abnormally widened beyond 0.12 second at 10 mEq/L. At this point they "merge" with the following T waves, resulting in a **"sine wave" QRS-ST-T pattern.**

ST Segments: Disappear at a serum potassium level of about 6 mEq/L.

T Waves: Become typically tall and peaked with a narrower than normal base at serum potassium levels of about 5.5-6.5 mEq/L.

Associated Arrhythmias:

- **Sinus arrest** (May occur at a serum potassium level of about 7.5 mEq/L.)
- **Cardiac standstill** (May occur at serum potassium levels of about 10 to 12 mEq/L.)
- **Ventricular fibrillation** (May occur at serum potassium levels of about 10 to 12 mEq/L.)

Hypokalemia

QRS Complexes: Begin to widen at a serum potassium level of about 3.0 mEq/L.

ST Segments: May become depressed by 1 mm or more.

T Waves: Begin to flatten at a serum potassium level of about 3.0 mEq/L and continue to become smaller as the **U waves** increase in size. The T waves may either merge with the U waves or become inverted.

U Waves: Begin to increase in size, becoming as tall as the T waves at a serum potassium level of about 3.0 mEq/L and, at about 2 mEq/L, becoming taller than the T waves. The U waves reach "giant" size and fuse with the T waves at 1 mEq/L.

QT Intervals: May appear to be prolonged when the U waves become prominent and fuse with the T waves but actually remain normal.

Serum potassium levels

A. normal (3.5 - 5.0 mEq/L)
B. about 3.0 mEq/L
C. 2.0 mEq/L
D. 1.0 mEq/L

Associated Arrhythmias:

- **Ventricular arrhythmias, including the torsade de pointes form of ventricular tachycardia** (May occur in hypokalemia in the presence of digitalis.)

Hypercalcemia

QT Intervals: Shorter than normal for the heart rate.

Hypocalcemia

ST Segments: Prolonged.

QT Intervals: Prolonged beyond the normal limits for the heart rate because of the prolonged ST segments.

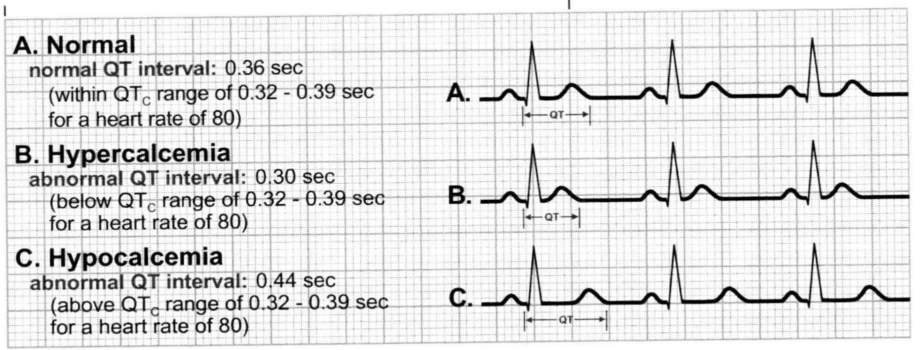

Serum calcium levels

A. normal (2.1 - 2.6 mEq/L)

B. hypercalcemia (>2.6 mEq/L)

C. hypocalcemia (<2.1 mEq/L)

Digitalis

PR Intervals: Prolonged over 0.2 second.

ST Segments: Depressed 1 mm or more in many of the leads, with a characteristic **"scooped-out" appearance.**

T Waves: May be flattened, inverted, or biphasic.

QT Intervals: Shorter than normal for the heart rate.

ST

QT

abnormal QT interval: 0.30 sec
(below QT_C range of 0.32 - 0.39 sec
for a heart rate of 80)

Effects of Digitalis Toxicity: Excessive administration of digitalis may cause the following **excitatory** and **inhibitory effects** on the heart and its electrical conduction system.

Excitatory effects include:

- **Premature atrial contractions**
- **Paroxysmal atrial tachycardia with block**
- **Paroxysmal junctional tachycardia**
- **Premature ventricular contractions**
- **Ventricular tachycardia**
- **Ventricular fibrillation**

Inhibitory effects include:

- **Sinus bradycardia**
- **Sinoatrial (SA) exit block**
- **Atrioventricular (AV) block**

Procainamide

PR Intervals: May be prolonged.

QRS Complexes:

Duration: May be increased beyond 0.12 second, a sign of procainamide toxicity.

R waves: May be decreased in amplitude.

ST Segments: May be depressed 1 mm or more.

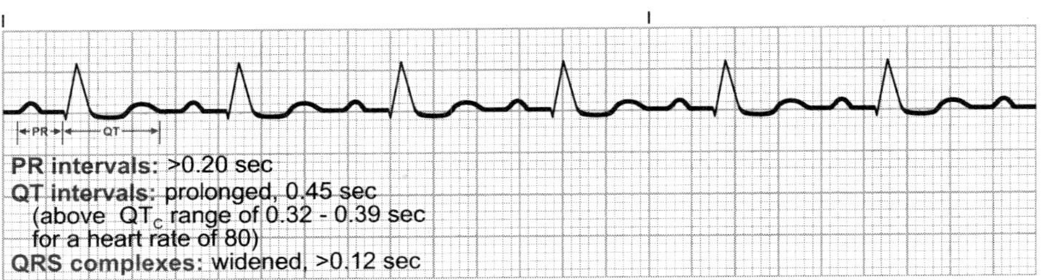

T Waves: May be decreased in amplitude, and occasionally widened and notched because of the appearance of a **U wave.**

QT Intervals: May occasionally be prolonged beyond the normal limits for the heart rate, a sign of procainamide toxicity.

Effects of Procainamide Toxicity: Excessive administration of procainamide may cause the following **excitatory** and **inhibitory effects** on the heart and its electrical conduction system.

Excitatory effects include:

- **Premature ventricular contractions**
- **Ventricular tachycardia in the form of torsade de pointes** (occurrence less common than in quinidine administration)
- **Ventricular fibrillation**

Inhibitory effects include:

- **Depression of myocardial contractility** which may cause **hypotension** and **congestive heart failure**
- **Atrioventricular (AV) block**
- **Ventricular asystole**

Quinidine

P Waves: May be wide, often notched.

PR Intervals: May be prolonged beyond normal.

QRS Complexes:

Duration: May be increased beyond 0.12 second, a sign of quinidine toxicity.

ST Segments: May be depressed 1 mm or more.

PR QT

PR intervals: >0.20 sec
QT intervals: prolonged, 0.45 sec (above QT_c range of 0.32 - 0.39 sec for a heart rate of 80)
QRS complexes: widened, >0.12 sec

T Waves: May be decreased in amplitude, wide, and notched, or they may be inverted. The notching is caused by the appearance of a **U wave** as the T wave widens.

QT Intervals: May be prolonged beyond the normal limits for the heart rate. **Prolongation of the QT interval** is a sign of quinidine toxicity.

Effects of Quinidine Toxicity: Excessive administration of quinidine may cause the following **excitatory** and **inhibitory effects** on the heart and its electrical conduction system.

Excitatory effects include:

- **Premature ventricular contractions**
- **Ventricular tachycardia in the form of torsade de pointes** (occurrence more common than in procainamide administration)
- **Ventricular fibrillation**

Inhibitory effects include:

- **Depression of myocardial contractility** which may cause **hypotension** and **congestive heart failure**
- **Sinoatrial (SA) exit block**
- **Atrioventricular (AV) block**
- **Ventricular asystole**

Chronic Obstructive Pulmonary Disease (COPD)

P Waves: **Right atrial enlargement** may be present.

QRS Complexes: Usually of low voltage. **Poor R-wave progression** across the precordium is usually present.

QRS Axis: May be **greater than +90°.**

Associated Arrhythmias:

- **Premature atrial contractions**
- **Wandering atrial pacemaker**
- **Multifocal atrial tachycardia**
- **Atrial flutter**
- **Atrial fibrillation**

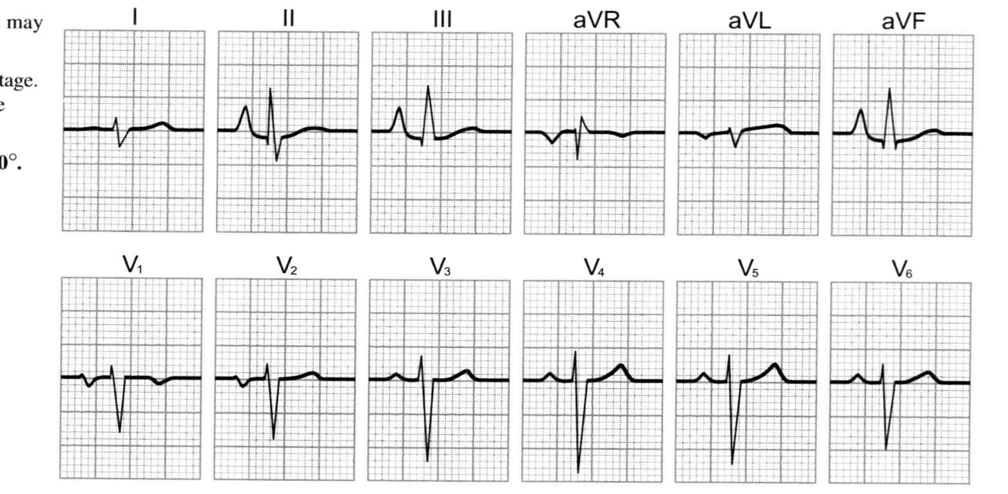

Cor Pulmonale

P Waves: **Right atrial enlargement** present.

QRS Complexes: **Right ventricular hypertrophy** present.

ST Segments/T Waves: **Right ventricular "strain" pattern** in leads V_1-V_2.

QRS Axis: **Greater than +90°.**

Associated Arrhythmias:

- **Premature atrial contractions**
- **Wandering atrial pacemaker**
- **Multifocal atrial tachycardia**
- **Atrial flutter**
- **Atrial fibrillation**

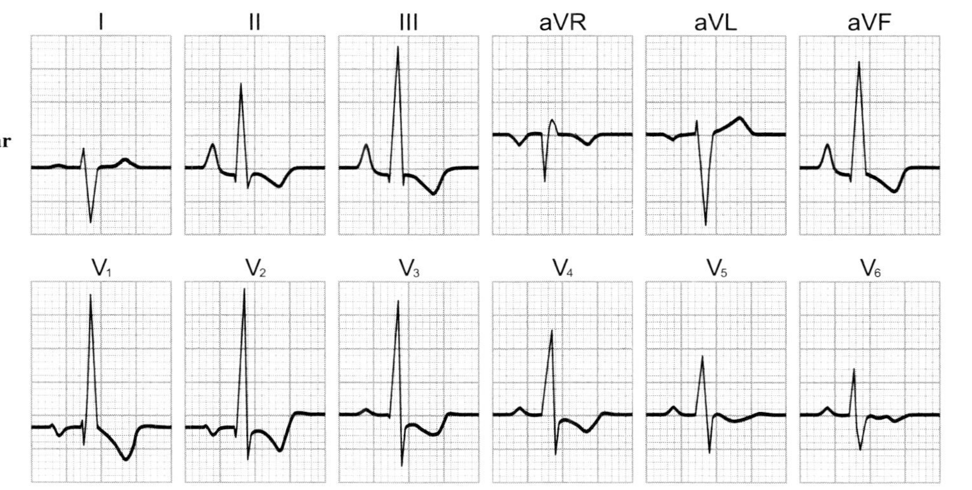

Pulmonary Embolism (Acute)

P Waves: **Right atrial enlargement** may be present.

QRS Complexes:

Q Waves: **Abnormal Q waves** in lead III.

S Waves: **Deep S waves** in lead I.

T Waves: **Inverted T waves** in lead III.

ST Segments/T Waves: **Right ventricular "strain" pattern** may be present in leads V_1-V_2.

QRS Pattern: An **$S_1Q_3T_3$ pattern** may occur acutely. In addition, a **right bundle branch block** may also occur.

QRS Axis: **Greater than +90°.**

Associated Arrhythmias:

- **Sinus tachycardia**

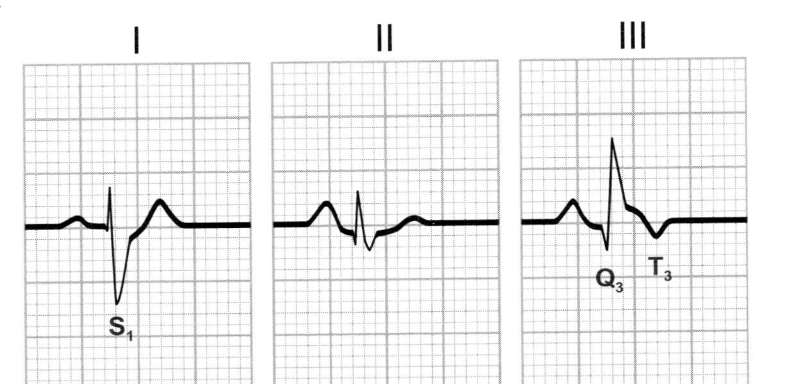

Causes of the Heart Chamber Enlargements and Electrolyte Imbalances Responsible for the ECG Changes Presented in Section IV

Cause of Right Atrial Enlargement (Right Atrial Dilatation and Hypertrophy): Increased pressure and/or volume in the right atrium, i.e., **right atrial overload,** commonly the result of pulmonary valve stenosis, tricuspid valve stenosis and insufficiency (relatively rare), and pulmonary hypertension from various causes. These include chronic obstructive pulmonary disease (COPD), status asthmaticus, pulmonary embolism, pulmonary edema, mitral valve stenosis or insufficiency, and congenital heart disease. The result of right atrial enlargement is, typically, a tall, symmetrically peaked P wave—the **P pulmonale.**

Cause of RVH: Increased pressure and/or volume in the right ventricle, i.e., **right ventricular overload,** commonly the result of pulmonary valve stenosis and other congenital heart defects (e.g., atrial and ventricular septal defects), tricuspid valve insufficiency (relatively rare), and pulmonary hypertension from various causes. These include chronic obstructive pulmonary disease (COPD), status asthmaticus, pulmonary embolism, pulmonary edema, and mitral valve stenosis or insufficiency.

Cause of Left Atrial Enlargement (Left Atrial Dilatation and Hypertrophy): Increased pressure and/or volume in the left atrium, i.e., **left atrial overload,** commonly the result of mitral valve stenosis and insufficiency, acute myocardial infarction, left heart failure, and left ventricular hypertrophy from various causes, such as aortic stenosis or insufficiency, systemic hypertension, and hypertrophic cardiomyopathy. The result of left atrial enlargement is, typically, a wide, notched P wave—the **P mitrale.** Such P waves may also result from a delay or block of the progression of the electrical impulses through the interatrial conduction tract between the right and left atria.

Cause of LVH: Increased pressure and/or volume in the left ventricle, i.e., **left ventricular overload,** commonly the result of mitral insufficiency, aortic stenosis or insufficiency, systemic hypertension, acute myocardial infarction, and hypertrophic cardiomyopathy.

Cause of Hyperkalemia: Excess of serum potassium above the normal levels of 3.5-5.0 milliequivalents per liter (mEq/L). The most common causes of hyperkalemia are kidney failure and certain diuretics (e.g., triamterene).

Cause of Hypokalemia: Deficiency of serum potassium below the normal levels of 3.5-5.0 milliequivalents per liter (mEq/L). The most common cause of hypokalemia is loss of potassium in body fluids through vomiting, gastric suction, and excessive use of diuretics. Hypokalemia may also result from low serum magnesium levels (hypomagnesemia). The ECG characteristics of hypomagnesemia, incidentally, resemble those of hypokalemia.

Cause of Hypercalcemia: Excess of serum calcium above the normal levels of 2.1-2.6 milliequivalents per liter (mEq/L) (or 4.25-5.25 mg/100 ml). Common causes of hypercalcemia include adrenal insufficiency, hyperparathyroidism, immobilization, kidney failure, malignancy, sarcoidosis, thyrotoxicosis, and vitamin A and D intoxication.

Cause of Hypocalcemia: Deficiency of serum calcium below the normal levels of 2.1-2.6 milliequivalents per liter (mEq/L) (or 4.25-5.25 mg/100 ml). Common causes of hypocalcemia include chronic steatorrhea, diuretics (such as furosemide or ethacrynic acid), hypomagnesemia (possibly because of release of parathyroid hormone), osteomalacia in adults and rickets in children, hypoparathyroidism, pregnancy, and respiratory alkalosis and hyperventilation.

Section V

Acute Myocardial Infarction

Locations of Myocardial Infarctions

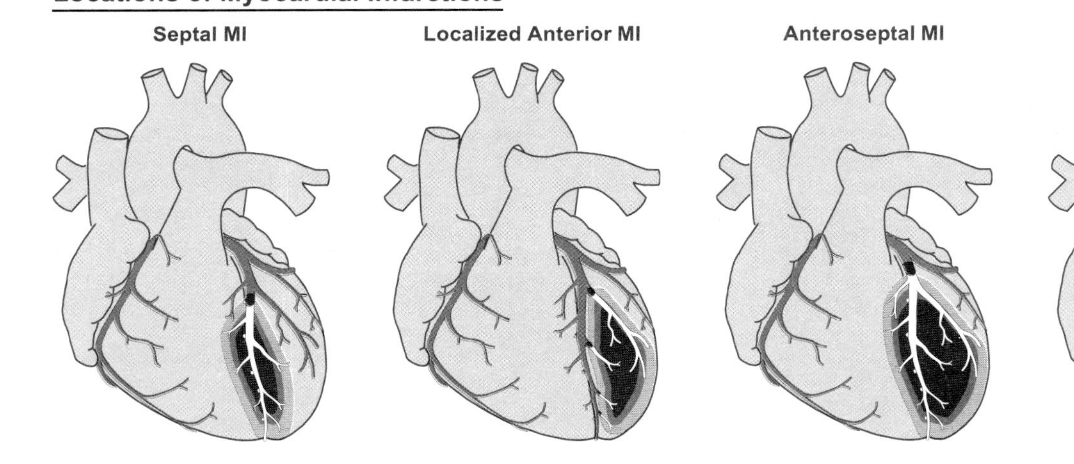

Arteries involved:

Septal MI	Localized Anterior MI	Anteroseptal MI	Lateral MI
Left anterior descending artery Septal perforator branches	Left anterior descending artery Diagonal branches	Left anterior descending artery Septal perforating branches Diagonal branches	Left anterior descending artery Diagonal branches Left circumflex artery Anterolateral marginal branch

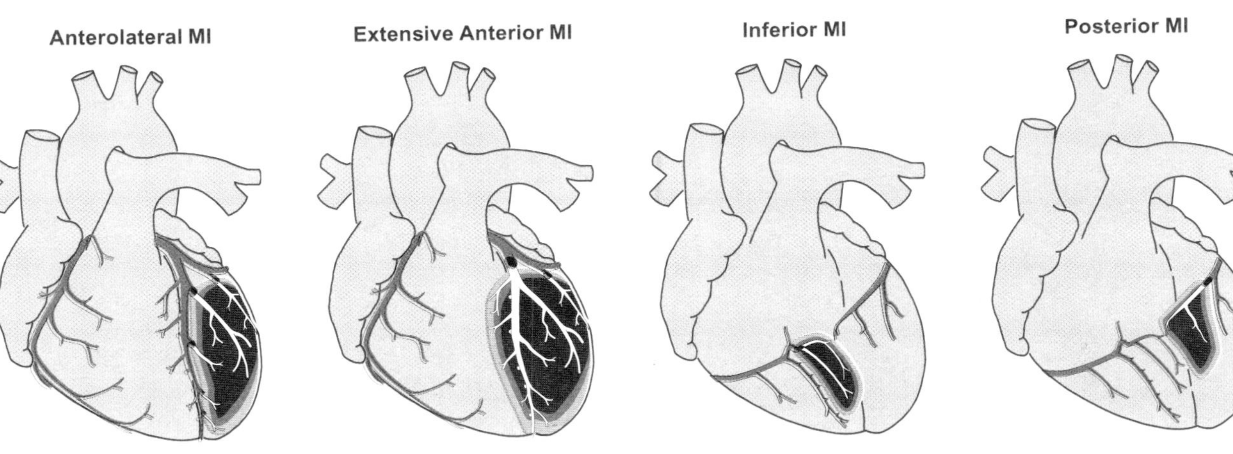

Arteries involved:

Left anterior descending artery
  Diagonal branches
Left circumflex artery
  Anterolateral marginal branch

Left anterior descending artery
Left circumflex artery
  Anterolateral marginal branch

Right coronary (or left circumflex) artery
  Posterior left ventricular branches

Distal left circumflex artery and/or its posterolateral branch

Septal Myocardial Infarction

EARLY

Phase 1: First Few Hours (0 to 2 Hours)

ECG Changes

In **facing leads V_1-V_2:**

- Absence of normal **"septal" r waves** in leads V_1-V_2, resulting in **QS waves** in these leads.
- **ST segment elevation** with **tall T waves** in leads V_1-V_2.

In **leads I, II, III, aVF, and V_4-V_6:**

- Absence of normal **"septal" q waves** where normally present in leads I, II, III, aVF, and V_4-V_6.

In **opposite leads II, III,** and **aVF:**

- No significant ECG changes in leads II, III, and aVF.

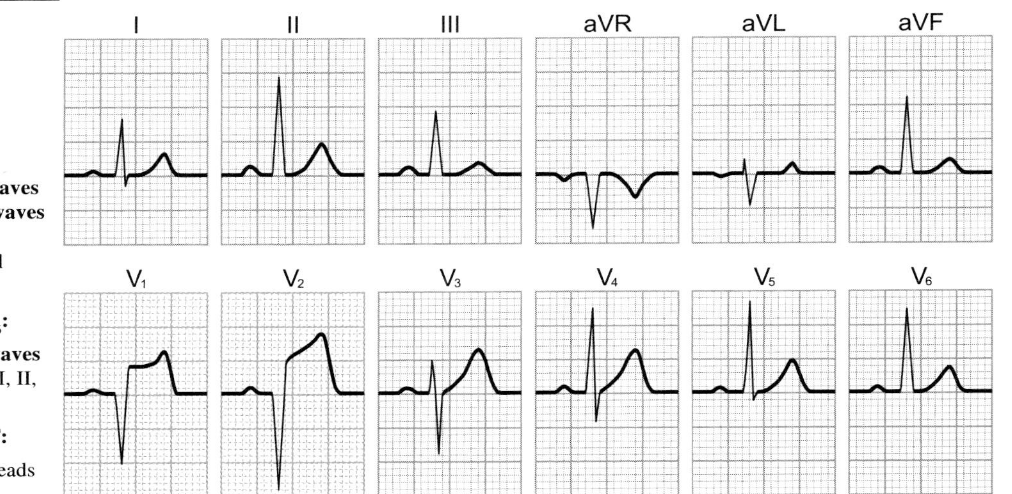

EARLY (CONT.)

Phase 2: First Day (2 to 24 Hours)

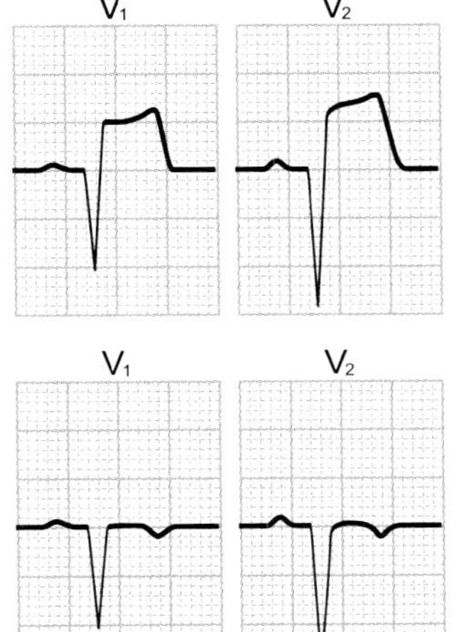

ECG Changes

In **facing leads V_1-V_2:**

- **Maximal ST segment elevation** in leads V_1-V_2.

LATE

Phase 3: Second and Third Day (24 to 72 Hours)

ECG Changes

In **facing leads V_1-V_2:**

- **QS complexes** with **T wave inversion** in leads V_1-V_2.
- Return of **ST segments to baseline** in leads V_1-V_2.

In **opposite leads II, III,** and **aVF:**

- No significant ECG changes in leads II, III, and aVF.

Anterior (Localized) Myocardial Infarction

EARLY

Phase 1: First Few Hours (0 to 2 Hours)

ECG Changes

In **facing leads V_3-V_4:**

- **ST segment elevation** with **tall T waves** and **taller than normal R waves** in leads V_3-V_4.

In **opposite leads II, III,** and **aVF:**

- No significant ECG changes in leads II, III, and aVF.

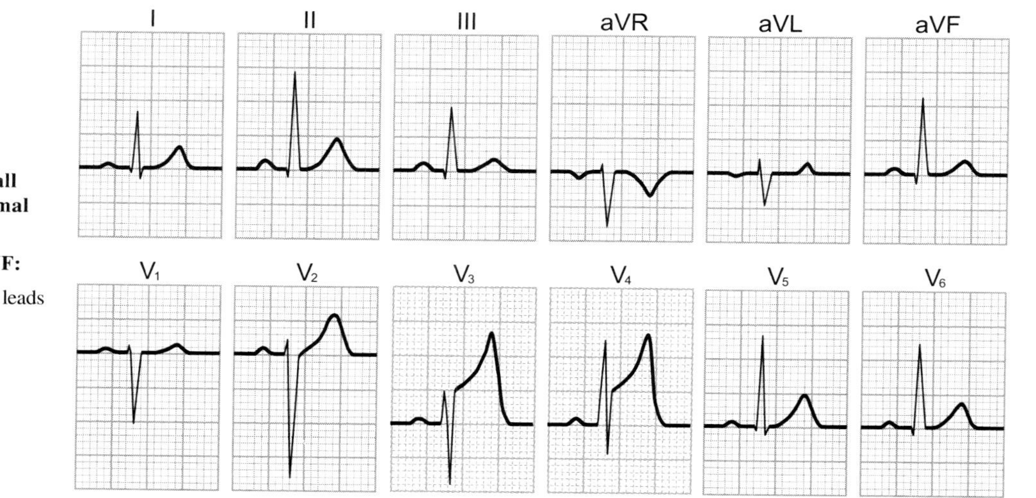

EARLY (CONT.)

Phase 2: First Day (2 to 24 Hours)

ECG Changes

In **facing leads V_3-V_4:**

- **Minimally abnormal Q waves** in leads V_3-V_4.
- **Maximal ST segment elevation** in leads V_3-V_4.

LATE

Phase 3: Second and Third Day (24 to 72 Hours)

ECG Changes

In **facing leads V_3-V_4:**

- **QS complexes** with **T wave inversion** in leads V_3- V_4.
- Return of **ST segments to baseline** in leads V_3- V_4.

In **opposite leads II, III,** and **aVF:**

- No significant ECG changes in leads II, III, and aVF.

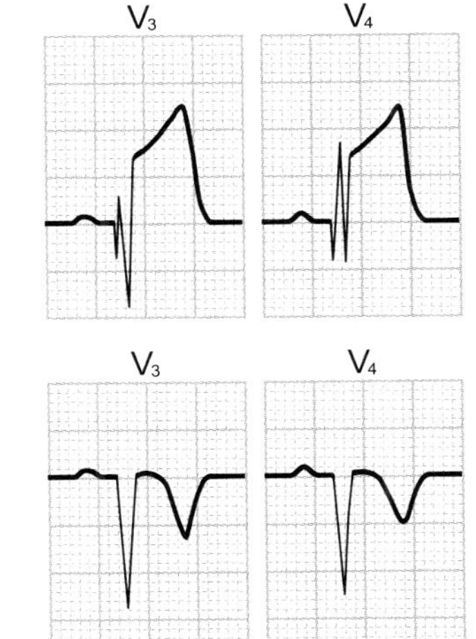

Anteroseptal Myocardial Infarction

EARLY

Phase 1: First Few Hours (0 to 2 Hours)

ECG Changes

In **facing leads V_1-V_4:**

- Absence of normal **"septal" r waves** in leads V_1-V_2, resulting in **QS waves** in these leads.
- **ST segment elevation** with **tall T waves** in leads V_1-V_4.
- **Taller than normal R waves** in leads V_3-V_4.

In **leads I, II, III, aVF, and V_4-V_6:**

- Absence of normal **"septal" q waves** where normally present in leads I, II, III, aVF, and V_4-V_6.

In **opposite leads II, III,** and **aVF:**

- No significant ECG changes in leads II, III, and aVF.

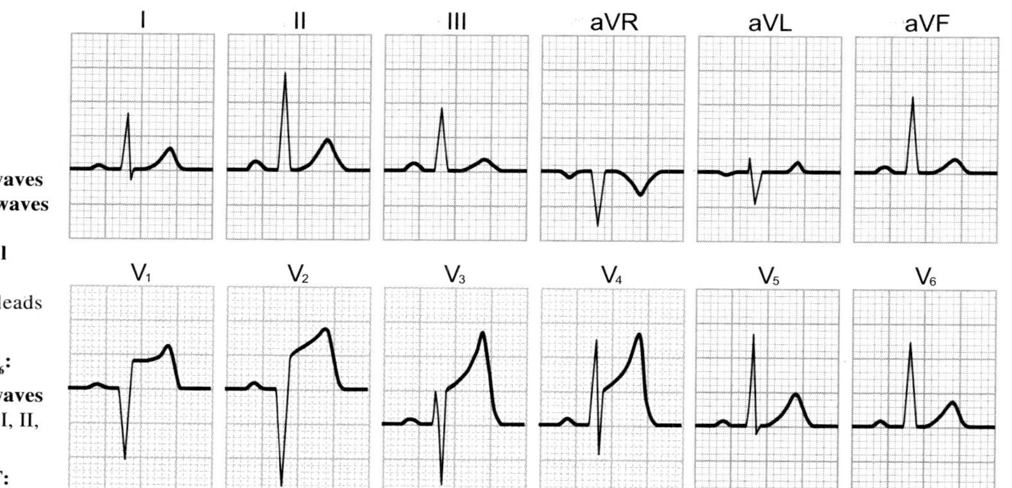

EARLY (CONT.)

Phase 2: First Day (2 to 24 Hours)

ECG Changes

In **facing leads V_1-V_4:**

- **Minimally abnormal Q waves** in leads V_3-V_4.
- **Maximal ST segment elevation** in leads V_1-V_4.

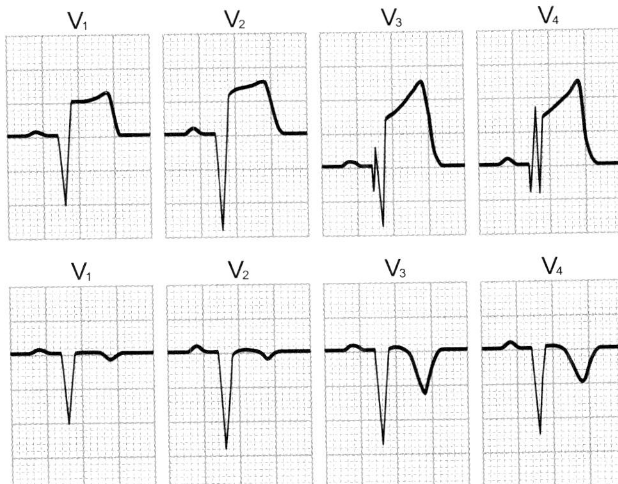

LATE

Phase 3: Second and Third Day (24 to 72 Hours)

ECG Changes

In **facing leads V_1-V_4:**

- **QS complexes** with **T wave inversion** in leads V_1-V_4.
- Return of **ST segments to baseline** in leads V_1-V_4.

In **opposite leads II, III,** and **aVF:**

- No significant ECG changes in leads II, III, and aVF.

Lateral Myocardial Infarction

EARLY

Phase 1: First Few Hours (0 to 2 Hours)

ECG Changes

In **facing leads I, aVL,** and **V_5-V_6**:

- **ST segment elevation** with **tall T waves** and **taller than normal R waves** in leads I, aVL, and lead V_5 or V_6 or both.

In **opposite leads II, III,** and **aVF:**

- **ST segment depression** in leads II, III, and aVF.

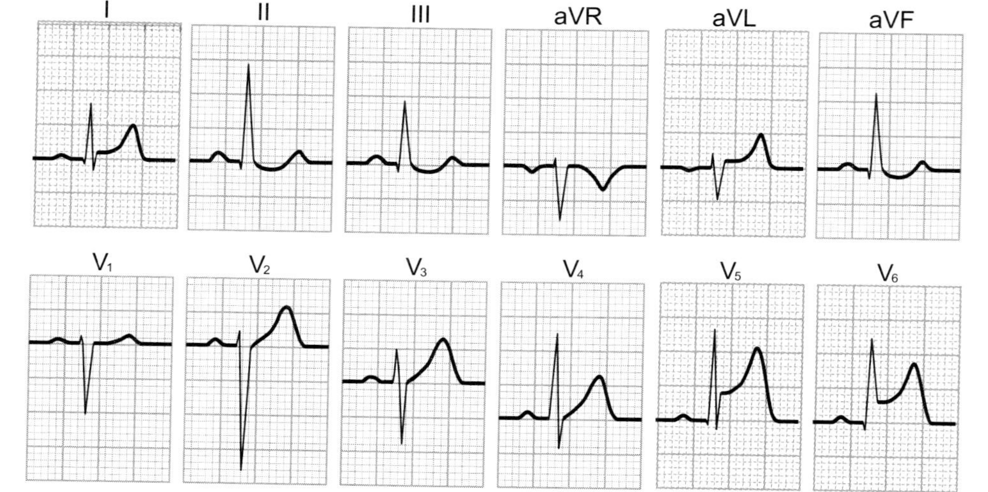

EARLY (CONT.)

Phase 2: First Day (2 to 24 Hours)

ECG Changes

In **facing leads I, aVL,** and **V_5-V_6**:

- **Minimally abnormal Q waves** in leads I and aVL and lead V_5 or V_6 or both.
- **Maximal ST segment elevation** in leads I and aVL and lead V_5 or V_6 or both.

LATE

Phase 3: Second and Third Day (24 to 72 Hours)

ECG Changes

In **facing leads I, aVL,** and **V_5-V_6**:

- **Abnormal Q waves** and **small R waves** with **T wave inversion** in leads I and aVL.
- **QS waves or complexes** with **T wave inversion** in lead V_5 or V_6 or both.
- Return of **ST segments to baseline** throughout.

In **opposite leads II, III,** and **aVF:**

- **Abnormally tall T waves** in leads II, III, and aVF.

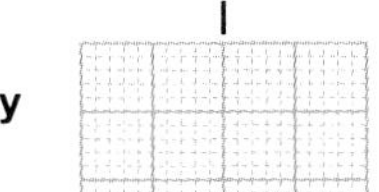

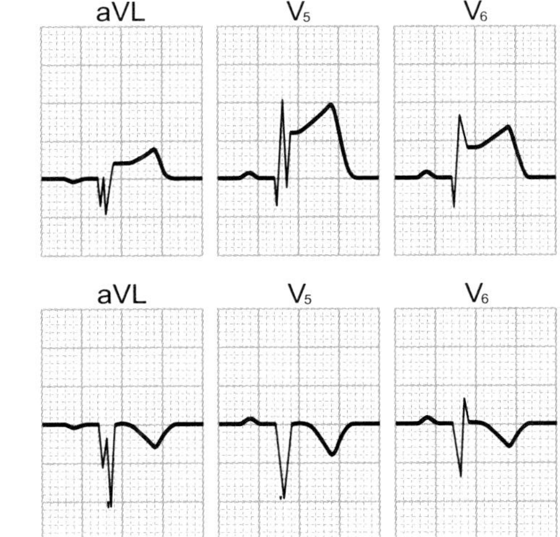

Anterolateral Myocardial Infarction

EARLY

Phase 1: First Few Hours (0 to 2 Hours)

ECG Changes

In **facing leads I, aVL,** and **V_3-V_6:**

- **ST segment elevation** with **tall T waves** and **taller than normal R waves** in leads I, aVL, and V_3-V_6.

In **opposite leads II, III,** and **aVF:**

- **ST segment depression** in leads II, III, and aVF.

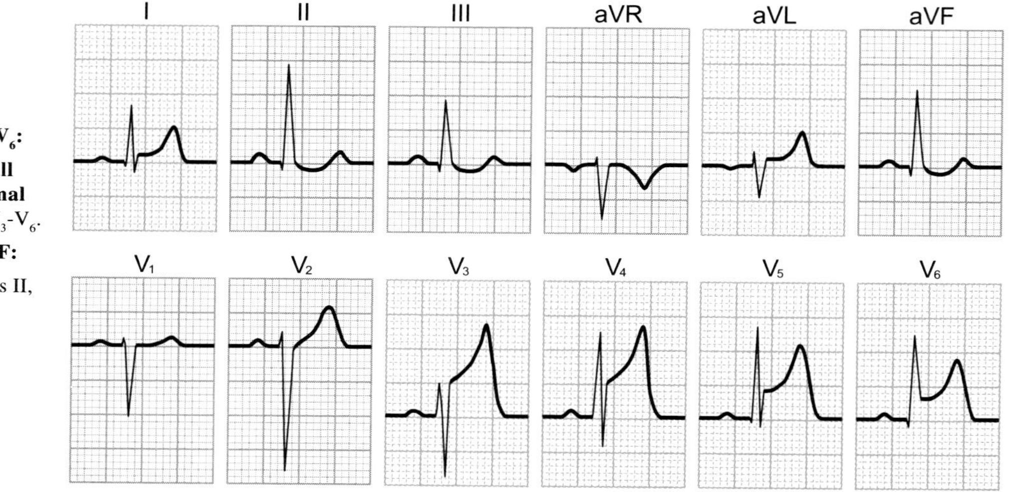

EARLY (CONT.)

Phase 2: First Day (2 to 24 Hours)

ECG Changes

In **facing leads I, aVL,** and **V_3-V_6:**

- **Minimally abnormal Q waves** in leads I, aVL, and V_3-V_6.
- **Maximal ST segment elevation** in leads I, aVL, and V_3-V_6.

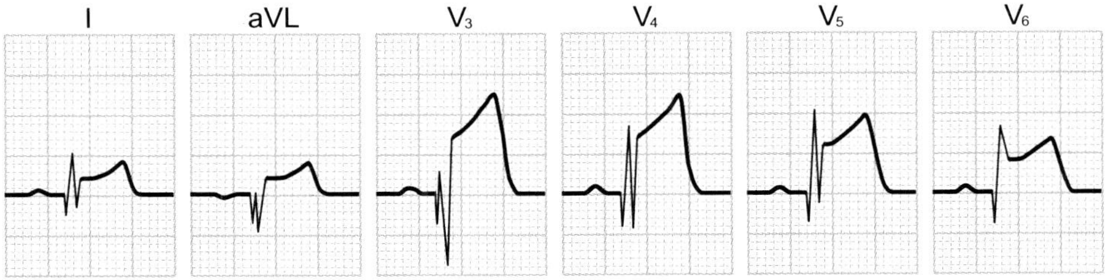

LATE

Phase 3: Second and Third Day (24 to 72 Hours)

ECG Changes

In **facing leads I, aVL,** and **V_3-V_6:**

- **Abnormal Q waves** and **small R waves** with **T wave inversion** in leads I and aVL.
- **QS waves or complexes** with **T wave inversion** in leads V_3-V_6.
- Return of **ST segments to baseline** throughout.

In **opposite leads II, III,** and **aVF:**

- **Abnormally tall T waves** in leads II, III, and aVF.

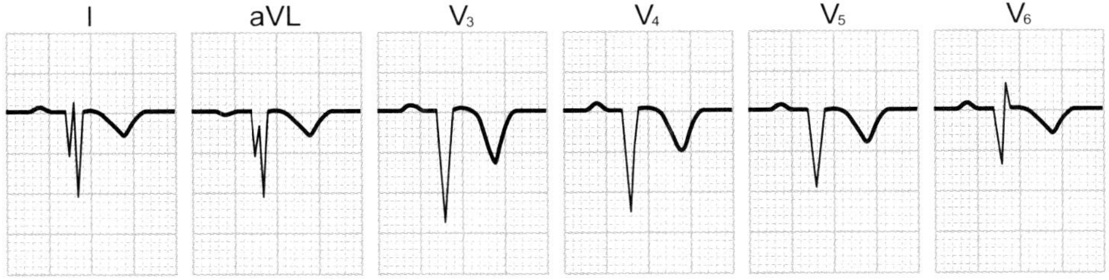

Extensive Anterior Myocardial Infarction

EARLY

Phase 1: First Few Hours (0 to 2 Hours)

ECG Changes

In **facing leads I, aVL,** and **V_1-V_6:**

- Absence of normal **"septal" r waves** in leads V_1-V_2, resulting in **QS complexes** in these leads.
- **ST segment elevation** with **tall T waves** in leads I, aVL, and V_1-V_6.
- **Taller than normal R waves** in leads I, aVL, and V_3-V_6.

In **leads I, II, III, aVF, and V_4-V_6:**

- Absence of normal **"septal" q waves** where normally present in leads I, II, III, aVF, and V_4-V_6.

In **opposite leads II, III,** and **aVF:**

- **ST segment depression** in leads II, III, and aVF.

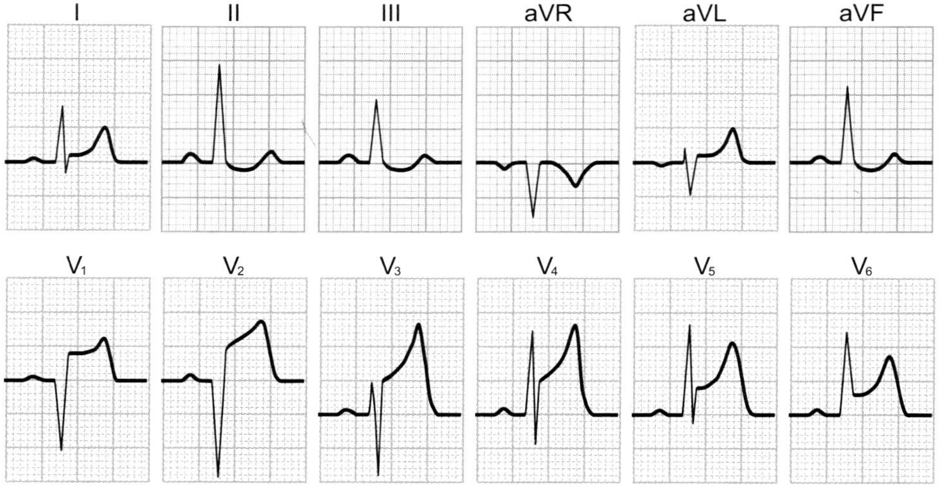

EARLY (CONT.)

Phase 2: First Day (2 to 24 Hours)

ECG Changes

In **facing leads I, aVL,** and **V_1-V_6:**

- **Minimally abnormal Q waves** in leads I, aVL, and V_3-V_6.
- **Maximal ST segment elevation** in leads I, aVL, and V_1-V_6.

LATE

Phase 3: Second and Third Day (24 to 72 Hours)

ECG Changes

In **facing leads I, aVL,** and **V_1-V_6:**

- **Abnormal Q waves** and **small R waves** with **T wave inversion** in leads I, aVL, and V_6.
- **QS waves or complexes** with **T wave inversion** in leads V_1-V_5 and some-times V_6.
- Return of **ST segments to baseline** throughout.

In **opposite leads II, III,** and **aVF:**

- **Abnormally tall T waves** in leads II, III, and aVF.

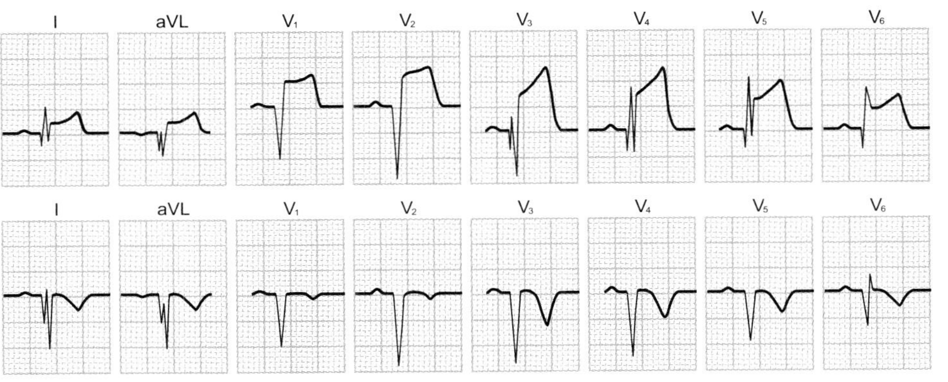

Inferior Myocardial Infarction

EARLY

Phase 1: First Few Hours (0 to 2 Hours)

ECG Changes

In **facing leads II, III,** and **aVF:**

- **ST segment elevation** with **tall T waves** and **taller than normal R waves** in leads II, III, and aVF.

In **opposite leads I** and **aVL:**

- **ST segment depression** in leads I and aVL.

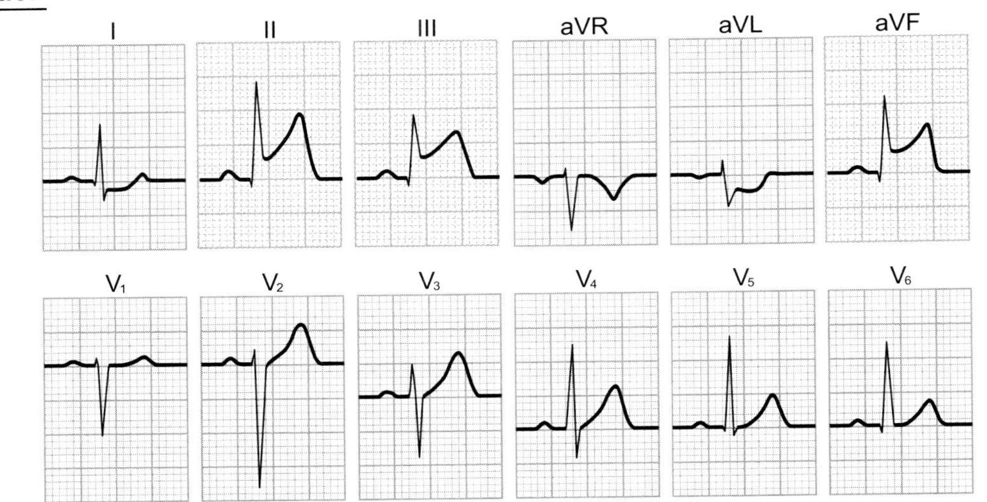

EARLY (CONT.)

Phase 2: First Day (2 to 24 Hours)

ECG Changes

In **facing leads II, III,** and **aVF:**

- **Minimally abnormal Q waves** in leads II, III, and aVF.
- **Maximal ST segment elevation** in leads II, III, and aVF.

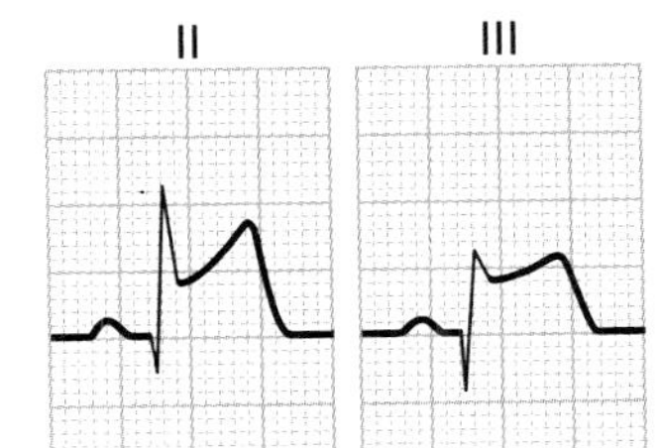

LATE

Phase 3: Second and Third Day (24 to 72 Hours)

ECG Changes

In **facing leads II, III,** and **aVF:**

- **QS waves or complexes** with **T wave inversion** in leads II, III, and aVF.
- Return of **ST segments to baseline** throughout.

In **opposite leads I** and **aVL:**

- **Abnormally tall T waves** in leads I and aVL.

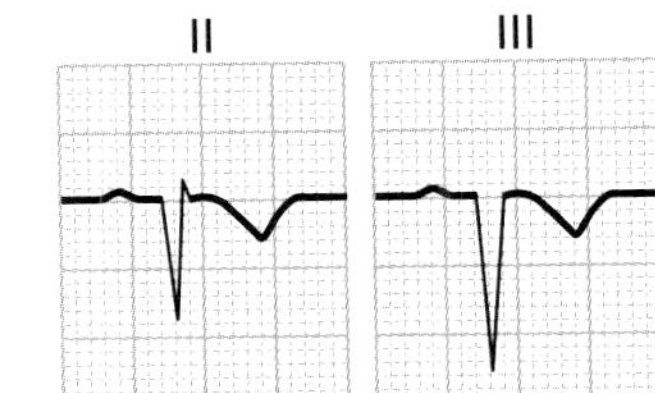

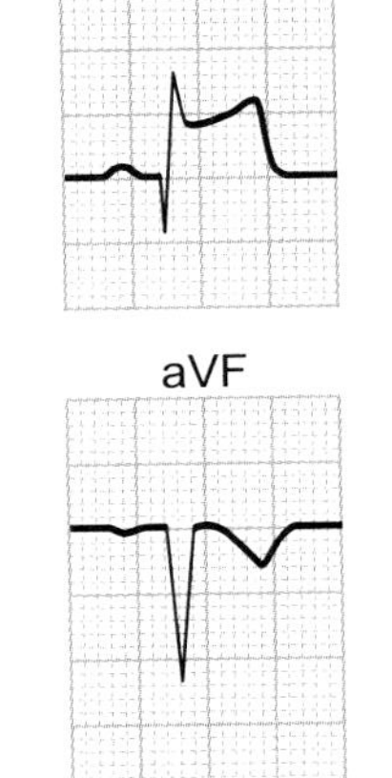

Posterior Myocardial Infarction

EARLY

Phase 1: First Few Hours (0 to 2 Hours)

ECG Changes

In **facing leads:** No facing leads present.

In **opposite leads V_1-V_4:**

- **ST segment depression** in leads V_1-V_4.

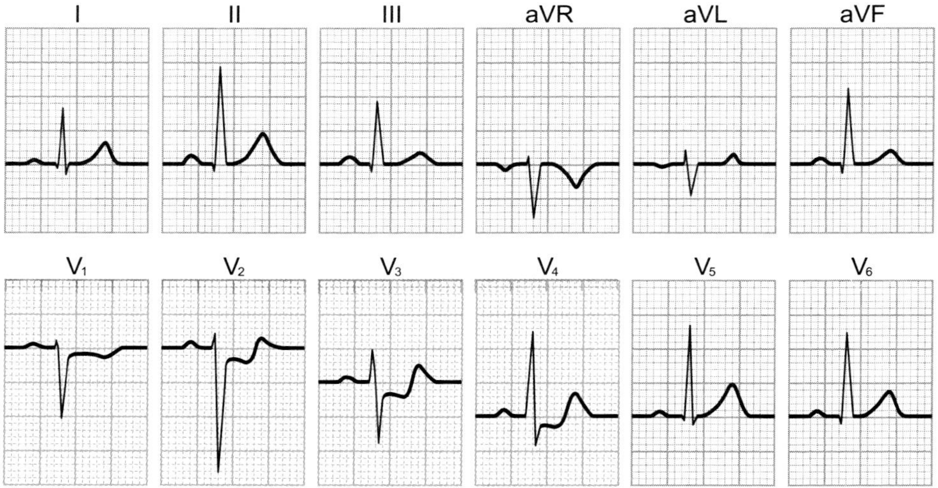

EARLY (CONT.)

Phase 2: First Day (2 to 24 Hours)

ECG Changes

In **facing leads:** No facing leads present.

In **opposite leads V_1-V_4:**

- **Maximal ST segment depression** in leads V_1-V_4.

LATE

Phase 3: Second and Third Day (24 to 72 Hours)

ECG Changes

In **facing leads:** No facing leads present.

In **opposite leads V_1-V_4:**

- **Large R waves** with **tall T waves** in leads V_1-V_4. The **R waves** in lead V_1 are **tall and wide (≥0.04 sec in width) with slurring and notching.**
- **Smaller than normal S waves** in lead V_1, resulting in a **R/S ratio of ≥1** in this lead.
- Return of **ST segments to baseline** in leads V_1-V_4.

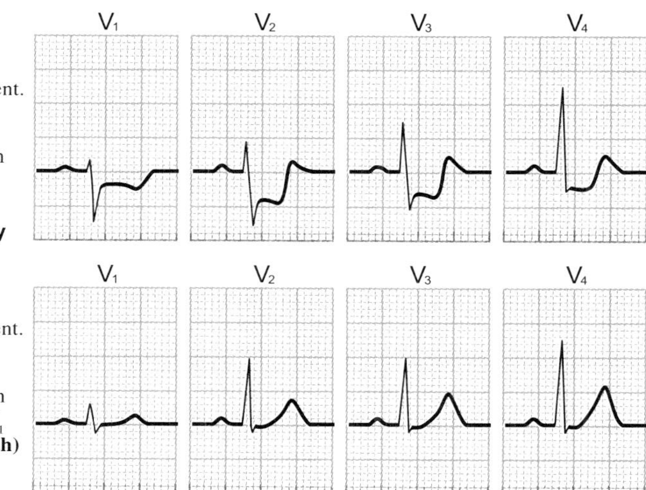

Appendix

ELECTRICAL CONDUCTION SYSTEM

CORONARY CIRCULATION

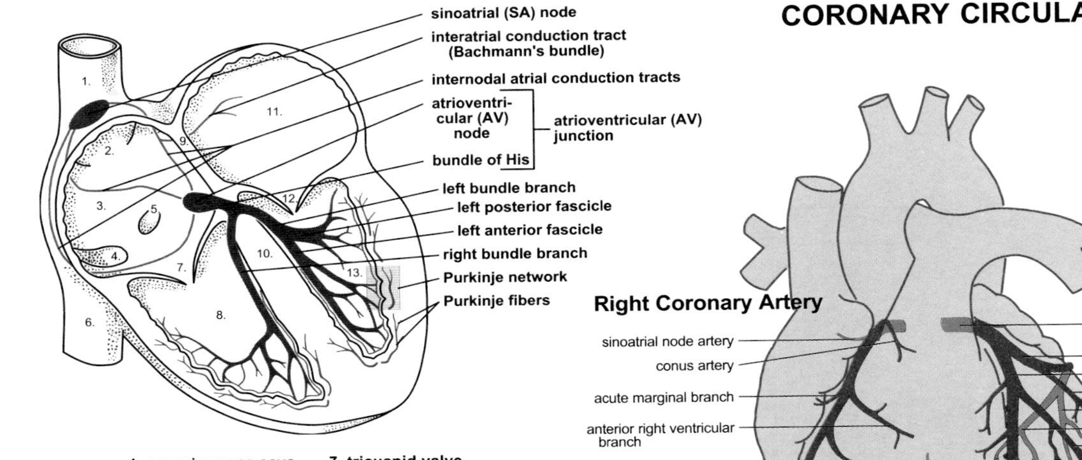

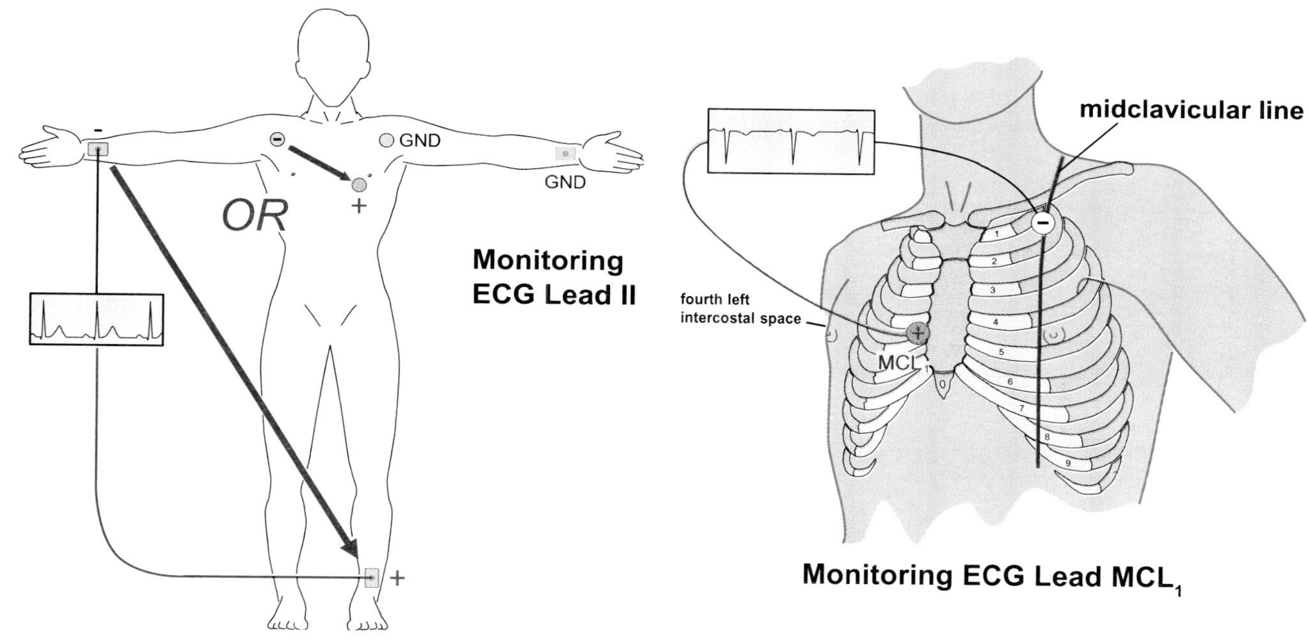

Monitoring
ECG Lead II

Monitoring ECG Lead MCL_1

The 12-Lead ECG

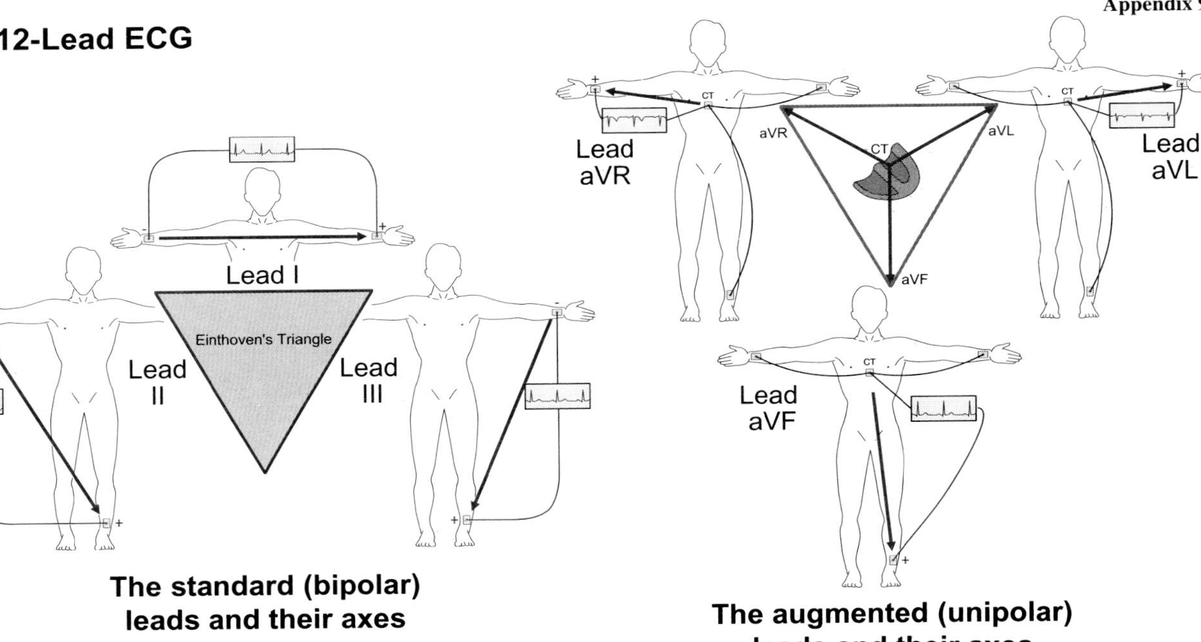

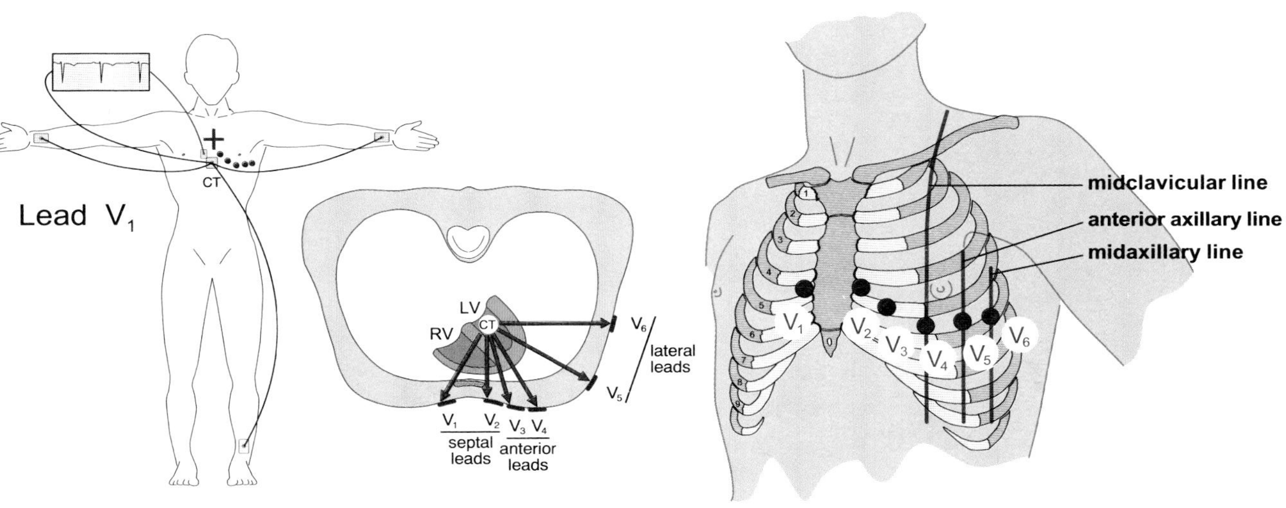

The precordial (unipolar) leads

Placement of precordial electrodes

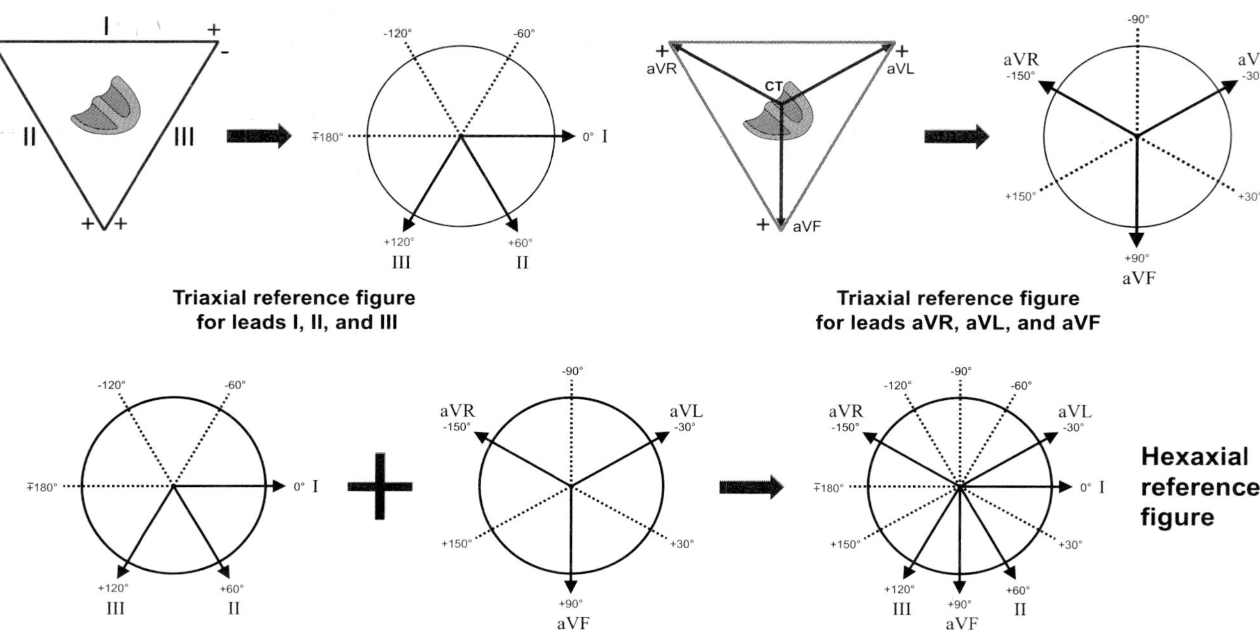

Triaxial reference figure for leads I, II, and III

Triaxial reference figure for leads aVR, aVL, and aVF

Hexaxial reference figure

The lead axes and their perpendiculars

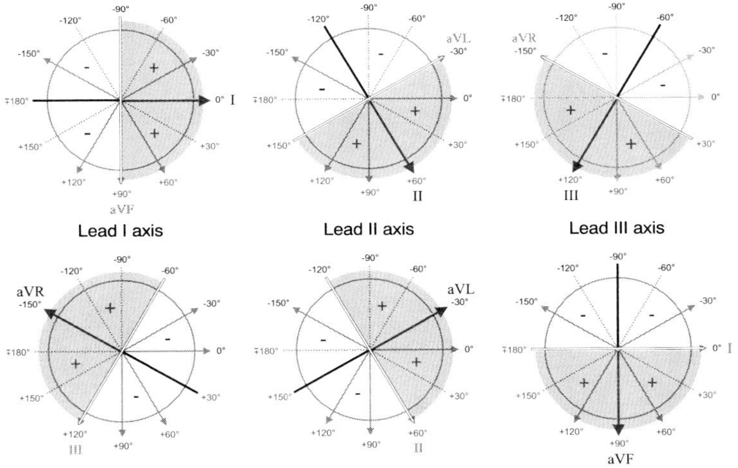

Lead I axis

Lead II axis

Lead III axis

Lead aVR axis

Lead aVL axis

Lead aVF axis

Legend:

- Positive half of the lead axis
- Negative half of the lead axis
- Perpendicular to the lead axis
- + Positive side of the perpendicular
- - Negative side of the perpendicular
- X Lead coincident with the perpendicular of a lead

Normal and abnormal QRS axes

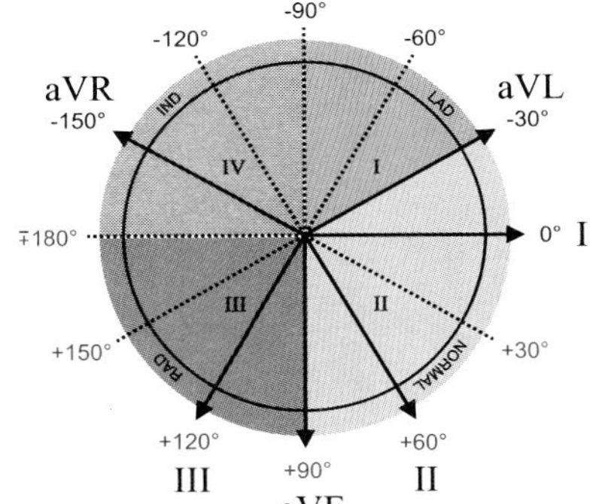

Normal	Normal QRS axis	-30° to +90°
LAD	Left axis deviation	-30° to -90°
RAD	Right axis deviation	+90° to +180°
IND	Indeterminate axis	-90° to -180°

The Three-lead Method of Determining the QRS Axis

If **lead I** is **positive** and:

A. **Leads aVF** and **II** are **predominantly positive,** the QRS axis is between **0°** and **+90°.**

B. **Lead aVF** is **predominantly negative,** and **lead II, predominantly positive,** the QRS axis is between **0°** and **-30°**.

C. **Lead aVF** is **predominantly negative,** and **lead II, equiphasic,** the QRS axis is exactly **-30°**.

D. **Leads aVF** and **II** are **predominantly negative,** the QRS axis is between **-30°** and **-90°.**

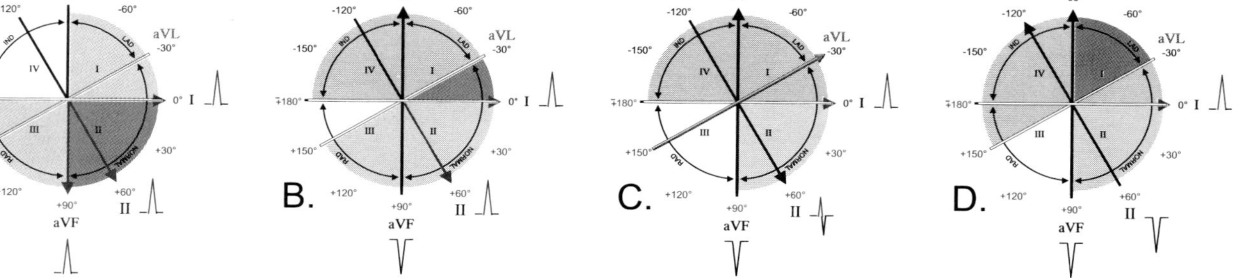

If **lead I** is **negative** and:

E.a. **Leads aVF** and **II** are **predominantly positive,** the QRS axis is between **+90°** and **+150°.**

E.b. If, in addition, **lead aVR** is also **predominantly positive,** the QRS axis is between **+120°** and **+150°.**

F. **Lead aVF** is **predominantly positive,** and **lead II, equiphasic,** the QRS axis is exactly **+150°**.

G. **Leads aVF** and **II** are **predominantly negative,** the QRS axis is between **-90°** and **-180°.**

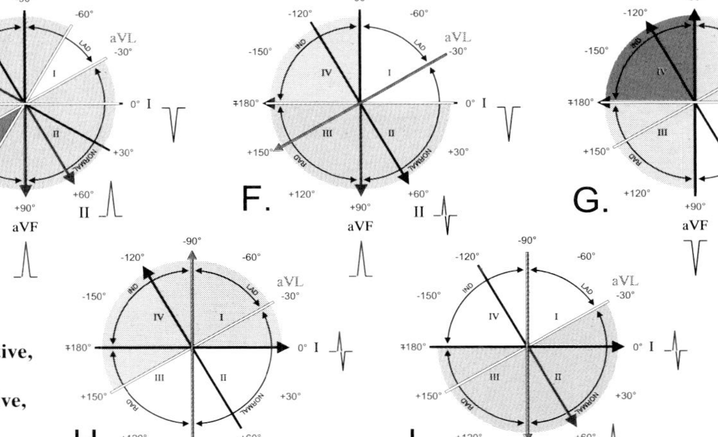

If **lead I** is **equiphasic** and:

H. **Leads aVF** and **II** are **predominantly negative,** the QRS axis is exactly **-90°.**

I. **Leads aVF** and **II** are **predominantly positive,** the QRS axis is exactly **+90°.**

Components of the Electrocardiogram

Waves

P Wave	**Normal Sinus P Wave** **Abnormal Sinus P Wave** **Ectopic P Wave (P Prime or P´)**
QRS Complex	**Normal QRS Complex** **Abnormal QRS Complex**
T Wave	**Normal T Wave** **Abnormal T Wave**
U Wave	

Intervals

PR Interval	**Normal PR Interval** **Abnormal PR Interval**
QT Interval	**Normal QT Interval** **Abnormal QT Interval**
R-R Interval	

Segments

ST Segment	**Normal ST Segment** **Abnormal ST Segment**
PR Segment	
TP Segment	

Normal Sinus P Wave

Significance: Represents **normal depolarization of the right and left atria,** which proceeds from right to left and downward.

Pacemaker Site: SA node.

ECG Characteristics:

Direction: Positive (upright) in lead II.

Duration: 0.10 second or less.

Amplitude: 0.5 to 2.5 mm in lead II.

Shape: Smooth and rounded.

P Wave-QRS Complex Relationship: Each normally followed by a QRS complex; **exception—AV block.**

PR Interval: May be normal (0.12 to 0.20 second) or abnormal (greater than 0.20 second or less than 0.12 second).

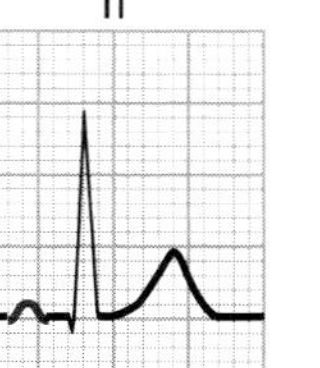

— = normal sinus P wave

Abnormal Sinus P Wave

Significance: Represents **depolarization of altered, damaged, or abnormal atria,** which proceeds from right to left and downward. Abnormal sinus P waves may be seen in:

- **Increased right atrial pressure** and **right atrial dilatation and hypertrophy (right atrial overload)** resulting from **chronic obstructive pulmonary disease, status asthmaticus, acute pulmonary embolism,** and **acute pulmonary edema** (tall and symmetrically peaked P waves **[P pulmonale]).**
- **Sinus tachycardia** (abnormally tall P waves).
- **Increased left atrial pressure** and **left atrial dilatation and hypertrophy (left atrial overload)** resulting from **hypertension, mitral and aortic valvular disease, acute myocardial infarction,** and **pulmonary edema secondary to left heart failure** (wide, notched P waves **[P mitrale]**).
- **Delay or block of the progression of electrical impulses through the interatrial conduction tract between the right and left atria** (wide, notched P waves **[P mitrale]**).

Pacemaker Site: SA node.

ECG Characteristics:

Direction: Positive (upright) in lead II.

Duration: May be normal (0.10 second or less) or greater than 0.10 second.

Amplitude: May be normal (0.5 to 2.5 mm) or greater than 2.5 mm in lead II. A **P pulmonale** is 2.5 mm or greater in amplitude.

Shape: May be tall and symmetrically peaked **(P pulmonale)** or wide and notched **(P mitrale).**

P Wave-QRS Complex Relationship: Each normally followed by a QRS complex; **exception—AV block.**

PR Interval: May be normal (0.12 to 0.20 second) or abnormal (greater than 0.20 second).

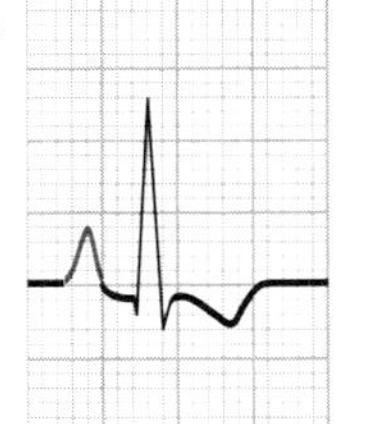

P pulmonale

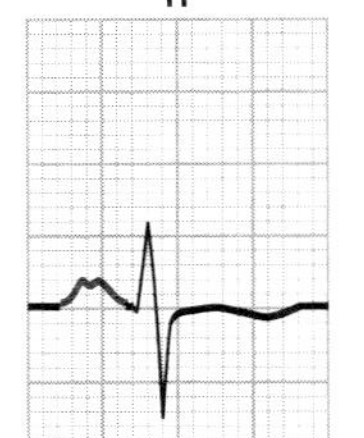

P mitrale

— = abnormal sinus P wave

Ectopic P Wave (P Prime or P´)

Significance: Represents **abnormal atrial depolarization occurring in an abnormal direction or sequence or both,** the direction and sequence depending on the pacemaker's location.

- **If the ectopic pacemaker is in the upper or middle part of the right atrium,** depolarization of the atria may occur in a normal direction (right to left and downward).
- **If the ectopic pacemaker is in the lower part of the right atrium near the AV node or in the left atrium or if it is in the AV junction or the ventricles,** in which case the electrical impulse travels upward through the AV junction into the atria **(retrograde conduction),** the atria depolarize from left to right and/or upward **(retrograde atrial depolarization).**

Ectopic P waves occur in various **atrial, junctional,** and **ventricular arrhythmias,** including:

- **Wandering atrial pacemaker**
- **Premature atrial contractions**
- **Nonparoxysmal atrial tachycardia**
- **Paroxysmal atrial tachycardia**
- **Premature junctional contractions**
- **Junctional escape rhythm**
- **Nonparoxysmal junctional tachycardia**
- **Paroxysmal junctional tachycardia**
- **Premature ventricular contractions (occasionally)**

Pacemaker Site: An ectopic pacemaker in the atria outside of the SA node or in the AV junction or ventricles.

ECG Characteristics:

Direction: May be **negative (inverted)** in lead II if the ectopic pacemaker is in the lower right atrium near the AV node, left atrium, AV junction, or ventricles or **positive (upright),** often resembling a normal sinus P wave, if the ectopic pacemaker is in any other part of the right atrium.

Duration: 0.10 second or less.

Amplitude: Usually less than 2.5 mm in lead II, but may be greater.

Shape: May be smooth and rounded, peaked, or dimple-shaped.

P Wave-QRS Complex Relationship: May precede, be buried in, or follow the QRS complex with which it is associated.

P´R/RP´ Interval: Relationship between site of ectopic pacemaker, type of interval, and duration:

- Upper or middle part of the right atria:
  P´R Interval—normal (0.12 to 0.20 second).
- Lower part of the atria, close to the AV node:
  P´R Interval—slightly less than 0.12 second.
- Upper part of the AV junction:
  P´R Interval—less than 0.12 second.
- Lower part of the AV junction or in the ventricles:
  RP´ Interval—usually less than 0.21 second.

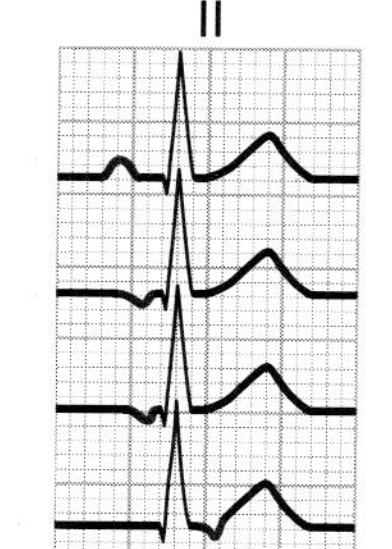

Normal QRS Complex

Significance: Represents **normal depolarization of the right and left ventricles,** which begins with the depolarization of the interventricular septum from left to right producing the Q wave and then continues with the depolarization of the ventricles from the endocardium to the epicardium producing the R and S waves.

Pacemaker Site: The SA node or an ectopic or escape pacemaker in the atria or AV junction.

ECG Characteristics:

Components: The QRS complex consists of one or more of the following **positive (upright) deflections** (the **R waves**) and **negative (inverted) deflections** (the **Q, S,** and **QS waves**).

- **R wave:** The first positive deflection in the QRS complex. Subsequent positive deflections that extends above the baseline are called **R prime (R´), R double prime (R´´),** and so forth.
- **Q wave:** The first negative deflection in the QRS complex not preceded by an R wave.
- **S wave:** The first negative deflection that extends below the baseline in the QRS complex following an R wave. Subsequent negative deflections are called **S prime (S´), S double prime (S´´),** and so forth.
- **QS wave:** A QRS complex that consists entirely of a single, large negative deflection.

Note: *Although there may be only one Q wave, there can be more than one R and S wave in the QRS complex.*

- **Notch:** A notch in the R wave is a negative deflection that does not extend below the baseline; a notch in the S wave is a positive deflection that does not extend above the baseline.

The **large waves** that form the major deflections are identified by **upper case letters (QS, R, S).** The **smaller waves** that are less than one-half the amplitude of the major deflections are identified by **lower case letters (q, r, s).** Thus, the ventricular depolarization complex can be described more accurately by using upper and lower case letters assigned to the waves, for example, **qR, Rs, qRs.**

Direction: May be predominantly positive (upright), predominantly negative (inverted), or equiphasic (partly positive, partly negative).

Duration:

QRS complex: 0.10 second or less (0.06 to 0.10 second) in adults and 0.08 second or less in children.
Q wave: 0.04 second or less.
Ventricular activation time (VAT): The time from the onset of the QRS complex to the peak of the R wave; normally 0.05 second or less, but may be greater than 0.05 second in left ventricular hypertrophy.

Amplitude: The amplitude of the R or S wave in the QRS complex in lead II may vary from 1 to 2 mm to 15 mm or more. The normal Q wave is less than 25% of the height of the succeeding R wave.

Shape: The QRS complex waves are generally narrow and sharply pointed.

Junction (J) Point: The end of the QRS complex at the point where the QRS complex becomes the ST segment.

Normal and Abnormal QRS Complexes

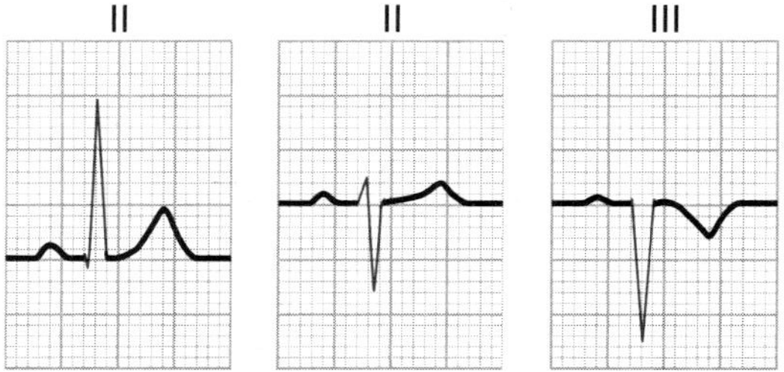

normal QRS complexes

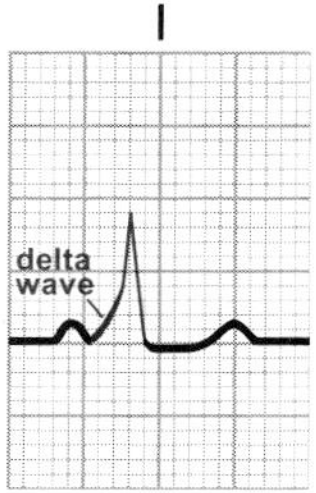

anomalous AV conduction

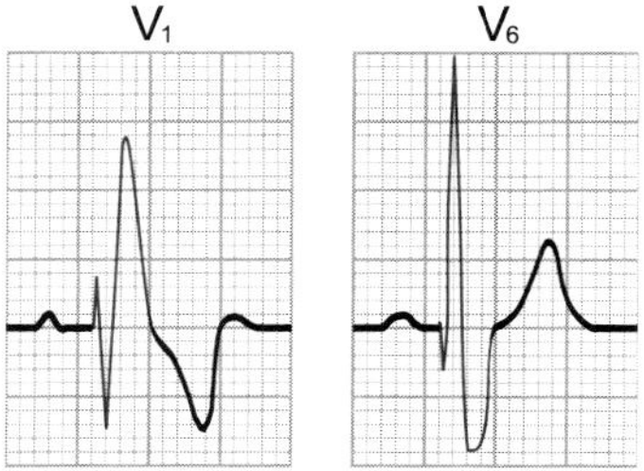

right bundle branch block

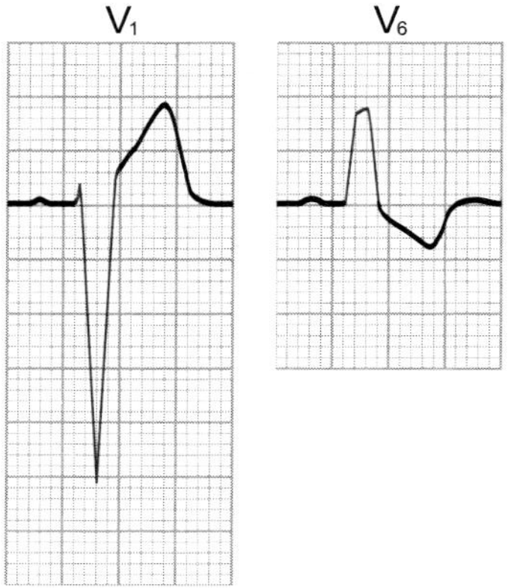

left bundle branch block

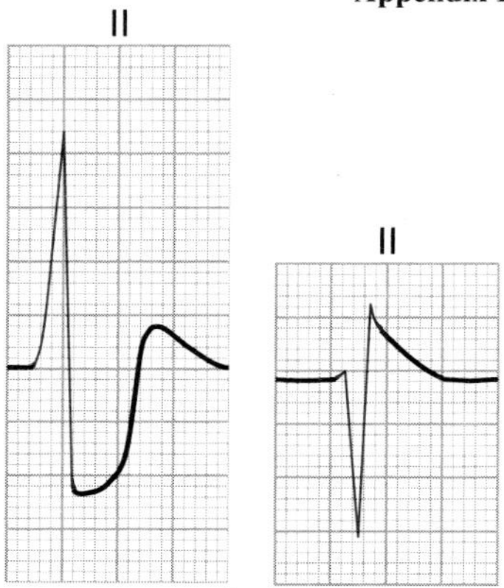

premature ventricular contractions

— = QRS complex

Abnormal QRS Complex

Significance: Represents **abnormal depolarization of the ventricles** which may result from one of the following:

- **Intraventricular conduction disturbance.** The most common forms are **right** and **left bundle branch block;** a less common form, a nonspecific, diffuse **intraventricular conduction defect (IVCD),** is seen in myocardial infarction, fibrosis, and hypertrophy; electrolyte imbalance, such as hypo- and hyperkalemia; and excessive administration of such cardiac drugs as quinidine and procainamide. May be seen in supraventricular rhythms and arrhythmias.
- **Aberrant ventricular conduction (aberrancy).** A temporary delay in the conduction of an electrical impulse through the bundle branches usually caused by the appearance of the electrical impulse at the bundle branches prematurely while they are still partially refractory and unable to conduct normally. The result is an abnormally wide QRS complex which may show a right or left bundle branch block pattern, a left anterior or posterior fascicular block pattern, or a combination of a right bundle branch block pattern and a left anterior or posterior fascicular block pattern. Aberrancy is most commonly seen in premature atrial and junctional contractions and supraventricular tachyarrhythmias.
- **Anomalous AV conduction (preexcitation syndrome).** Abnormal conduction of electrical impulses from the atria to the ventricles via an accessory pathway bypassing the AV junction. This commonly results in a shorter than normal PR interval **(0.09-0.12 sec)** and a wide QRS complex **(0.10 sec or more)** with an initial slurring of the upward slope of the R wave (the **delta wave**), the result of premature depolarization of a portion of one of the ventricles, all of which is characteristic of the **Wolff-Parkinson-White (WPW) syndrome.** Anomalous AV conduction may be seen in sinus and atrial rhythms and arrhythmias and in supraventricular tachyarrhythmias.
- **Ventricular arrhythmias.** Arrhythmias which originate in a **ventricular ectopic or escape pacemaker** located in the bundle branches, Purkinje network, or ventricular myocardium.

ECG Characteristics:

Components: The same as in normal QRS complexes. In addition, if anomalous AV conduction is present, an initial **delta wave** is usually present.

Direction: May be predominantly positive (upright), predominantly negative (inverted), or equiphasic (partly positive, partly negative).

Duration: Greater than 0.10 second.

Amplitude: Varies from 1 to 2 mm to 20 mm or more.

Shape: Varies widely in shape, from one that appears quite normal, i.e., narrow and sharply pointed (as in incomplete bundle branch block and aberrant ventricular conduction and in ventricular arrhythmias arising in the bundle branches), to one that is wide and bizarre, slurred and notched (as in complete bundle branch block and aberrant ventricular conduction and in ventricular arrhythmias arising in the Purkinje network and ventricular myocardium).

Normal T Wave

Significance: Represents **normal repolarization of the ventricles,** which proceeds from the epicardium to the endocardium.

ECG Characteristics:

Direction: **Positive (upright)** in lead II.

Duration: 0.10 to 0.25 second or greater.

Amplitude: Less than 5 mm in standard leads.

Shape: Sharply or bluntly rounded and slightly asymmetrical, the first, upward part being longer than the second, downward part.

T Wave-QRS Complex Relationship: Always follows the QRS complex.

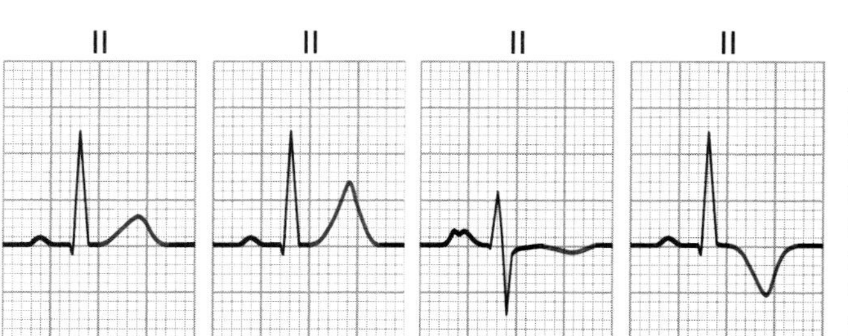

Abnormal T Wave

Significance: Represents **abnormal ventricular repolarization** which may proceed **(a)** from the epicardium to the endocardium but at a slower rate than normal, producing an **abnormally tall, upright T wave in lead II,** or **(b)** from the endocardium to the epicardium, producing a **negative T wave in lead II. Abnormal ventricular repolarization** may occur in the following:

- **Myocardial ischemia, acute myocardial infarction, myocarditis, pericarditis.**
- **Ventricular enlargement (hypertrophy).**
- **Electrolyte imbalance (e.g., excess serum potassium).**
- **Administration of certain cardiac drugs (e.g., quinidine, procainamide).**
- **Bundle branch block and ectopic ventricular arrhythmias.**
- **In athletes and in persons who are hyperventilating.**

ECG Characteristics:

Direction: May be positive (upright) and abnormally tall or low, negative (inverted), or biphasic (partially positive and partially negative) in lead II. The abnormal T wave may or may not be in the same direction as that of the normal QRS complex. The T wave following an abnormal QRS complex is almost always opposite in direction to it and abnormally wide and tall or deeply inverted.

Duration: 0.10 to 0.25 second or greater.

Amplitude: Variable.

Shape: May be rounded, blunt, sharply peaked, wide, or notched.

U Wave

Significance: Probably represents the **final stage of repolarization of a small segment of the ventricles** (such as the papillary muscles or ventricular septum) after most of the right and left ventricles have been repolarized.

Abnormally tall U waves may be present in:

- **Hypokalemia**
- **Cardiomyopathy, left ventricular hypertrophy**
- **Diabetes**
- **Administration of digitalis, quinidine, and procainamide**

ECG Characteristics:

Location: The downward slope of the T wave or following it.

Direction: Normally, positive (upright), the same direction as that of the preceding normal T wave in lead II. Abnormal U waves may be positive (upright) or negative (inverted).

Duration: Usually not determined.

Amplitude: Normally less than 2 mm and always smaller than that of the preceding T wave in lead II. A U wave taller than 2 mm is considered to be abnormal.

Shape: Rounded and symmetrical.

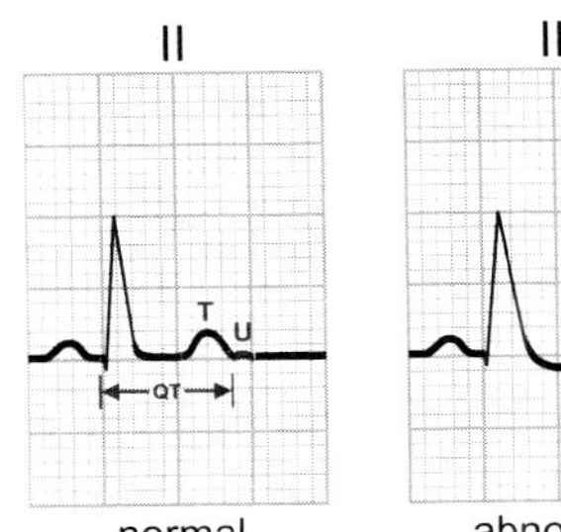

— = U wave

Normal QT Interval

Significance: Represents the **time between the onset of depolarization and the end of repolarization of the ventricles,** that is, the **refractory period of the ventricles,** and indicates that ventricular repolarization is normal.

ECG Characteristics:

Onset and End: Begins with the onset of the QRS complex and ends with the end of the T wave.

Duration: Dependent on the heart rate, being shorter when the heart rate is fast and longer when the heart rate is slow. Normally, the QT interval is somewhat less then half of the preceding R-R interval, one that is greater than half is abnormal, and one that is about half is "borderline." The QT intervals may be equal or unequal in duration depending on the underlying rhythm. The average duration of the QT interval normally expected at a given heart rate, the **corrected QT interval** (or **QTc**), and the normal range of 10% above and 10% below the average value are shown in the table to the right.

Note: The determination of the QT interval should be made in the lead where the T wave is most prominent and not deformed by a U wave, and should not include the U wave. Furthermore, the measurement of the QT interval assumes that the duration of the QRS complex is normal with an average value of 0.08 second. If the QRS is widened beyond 0.08 second for any reason, the excess widening beyond 0.08 second must be subtracted from the actual measurement to obtain the correct QT interval.

QTc Intervals

Heart Rate/min	R-R Interval (sec)	QTc (sec) and Normal Range
40	1.5	0.46 (.41-.51)
50	1.2	0.42 (.38-.46)
60	1.0	0.39 (.35-.43)
70	0.86	0.37 (.33-.41)
80	0.75	0.35 (.32-.39)
90	0.67	0.33 (.30-.36)
100	0.60	0.31 (.28-.34)
120	0.50	0.29 (.26-.32)
150	0.40	0.25 (.23-.28)
180	0.33	0.23 (.21-.25)
200	0.30	0.22 (.20-.24)

Abnormal QT Interval

Significance: Represents an **abnormal rate of ventricular repolarization,** either **slower** or **more rapid** than normal. An **abnormally prolonged QT interval,** one that exceeds the average QT interval for any given heart rate by 10 percent, indicates slowing of ventricular repolarization. This can occur in:

- **Electrolyte imbalance (hypokalemia and hypocalcemia).**
- **Excess of certain drugs (quinidine, procainamide, disopyramide, amiodarone, phenothiazines, and tricyclic antidepressants).** The prolongation of the QT interval following administration of excessive amounts of such antiarrhythmic agents as quinidine, procainamide, and disopyramide, may provoke the appearance of **torsade de pointes.**
- **Liquid protein diets.**
- **Pericarditis, acute myocarditis, acute myocardial infarction,** and **left ventricular hypertrophy.**
- **Hypothermia.**
- **Central nervous system disorders (e.g., subarachnoid hemorrhage, intracranial trauma).**
- **Without a known cause (idiopathic).**
- **Bradyarrhythmias (e.g., marked sinus bradycardia, third-degree AV block with slow ventricular escape rhythm).**

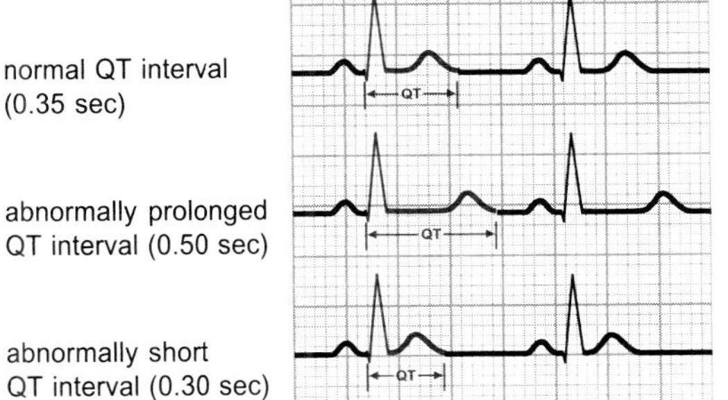

An **abnormally short QT interval,** one that is less than the average QT interval for any given heart rate by 10 percent, represents an increase in the rate of repolarization of the ventricles. This can occur in:

- **Digitalis therapy.**
- **Hypercalcemia.**

ECG Characteristics:

Onset and End: The same as those of a normal PR interval.

Duration: Greater or less than the average QT interval for any given heart rate by 10 percent.

R-R Interval

Significance: Represents the **time between two successive ventricular depolarizations** during which the atria and ventricles contract and relax once, i.e., **one cardiac cycle.**

ECG Characteristics:

Onset and End: Begins with the peak of one R wave and ends with the peak of the succeeding R wave.

Duration: Dependent on the heart rate, being shorter when the heart rate is fast and longer when the heart rate is slow (Example: heart rate 120, R-R interval 0.50 second; heart rate 60, R-R interval 1.0 second). The R-R intervals may be equal or unequal in duration depending on the underlying rhythm.

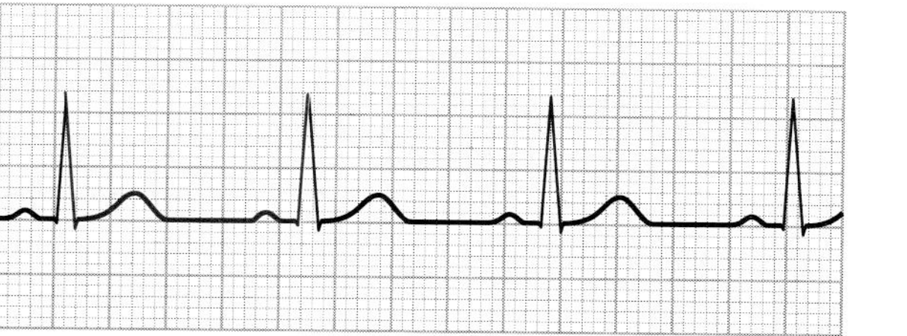

— = R-R interval

Normal PR Interval

Significance: Represents the **time from the onset of atrial depolarization to the onset of ventricular depolarization** during which the electrical impulse progresses normally and without delay from the SA node through the internodal atrial conduction tracts, AV node, bundle of His, bundle branches, and Purkinje network to the ventricular myocardium. The PR interval includes the P wave and PR segment.

ECG Characteristics:

Onset and End: Begins with the onset of the P wave and ends with the onset of the QRS complex.

Duration: Varies from 0.12 to 0.20 second, depending on the heart rate. Normally, it is shorter when the heart rate is fast and longer when the heart rate is slow (Example: heart rate 120, PR interval 0.16 second; heart rate 60, PR interval 0.20 second).

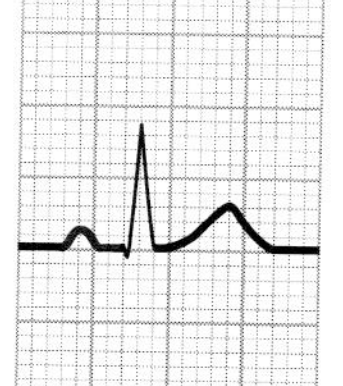

— = PR interval

normal PR interval

Abnormal PR Interval

Significance: Represents the abnormal progression of the electrical impulse from the SA node through the internodal atrial conduction tracts, AV node, bundle of His, bundle branches, and Purkinje network to the ventricular myocardium. It may be **greater than 0.20 second** or **less than 0.12 second.**

- When **greater then 0.20 second,** it represents **delayed progression of the electrical impulse through the AV node, bundle of His, or, rarely, the bundle branches.**
- When **less than 0.12 second,** it represents either:

  (a) the origination of the electrical impulse in an ectopic pacemaker in the atria close to the AV node or in the AV junction (in which case the P waves are commonly negative (inverted) in lead II),

  OR

  (b) the progression of the electrical impulse from the atria to the ventricles through an abnormal conduction pathway which bypasses the AV junction (the accessory pathway), depolarizing the ventricles earlier than usual—anomalous AV conduction (or the **preexcitation syndrome**). In anomalous AV conduction, the P waves may be positive (upright) or negative (inverted) in lead II and the QRS complexes, either **(1) wide, abnormally shaped** with a **delta wave,** the slurring of the onset of the QRS complex, (the **Wolff-Parkinson-White [WPW] syndrome**) or **(2) normal** (the **Lown-Ganong-Levine syndrome**).

ECG Characteristics:

Onset and End: The same as those of a normal PR interval.

Duration: May be greater than 0.20 second or less than 0.12 second.

abnormally prolonged PR interval

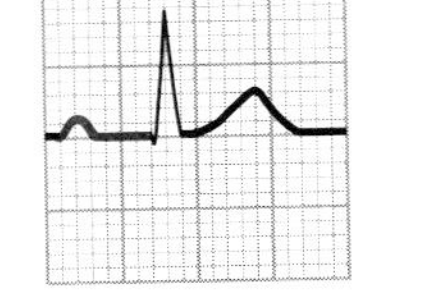

abnormally short PR interval

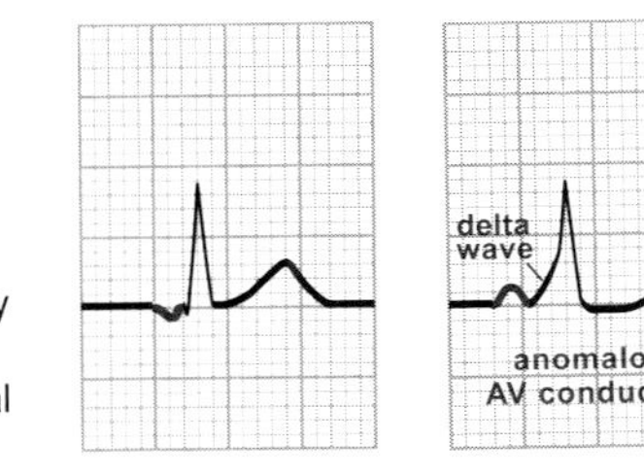

— = PR interval

Normal ST Segment

Significance: Represents the **early part of normal repolarization of the right and left ventricles.**

ECG Characteristics

Onset and End: Begins with the end of the QRS complex, the **"junction"** or **"J" point,** and ends with the onset of the T wave.

Duration: 0.20 second or less, depending on the heart rate, being shorter when the heart rate is fast and longer when the heart rate is slow.

Amplitude: Normally flat (isoelectric), but may be slightly elevated or depressed by **less than 1.0 mm, 0.08 second (2 small squares)** after the **J point** of the QRS complex and still be normal.

Appearance: If slightly elevated, may be flat, concave, or arched. If slightly depressed, may be flat, sagging, or downsloping.

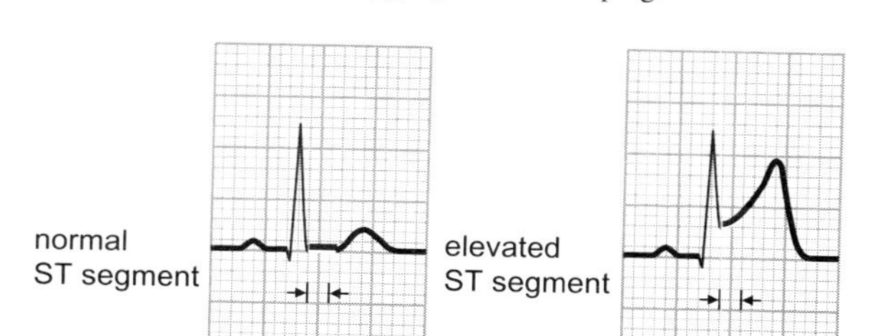

Abnormal ST Segment

Significance: Represents the **early part of abnormal repolarization of the right and left ventricles,** a common consequence of coronary artery disease (myocardial ischemia, acute myocardial infarction). It is also present in ventricular fibrosis or aneurysm, pericarditis, left ventricular enlargement (hypertrophy), and administration of digitalis.

ECG Characteristics

Onset and End: Same as those of a normal ST segment.

Duration: 0.20 second or less, depending on the heart rate.

Amplitude: Elevated or depressed **1.0 mm or more, 0.08 second (2 small squares)** after the **J point** of the QRS complex.

Appearance: If elevated, may be flat, concave, or arched. If depressed, may be flat, upsloping, or downsloping.

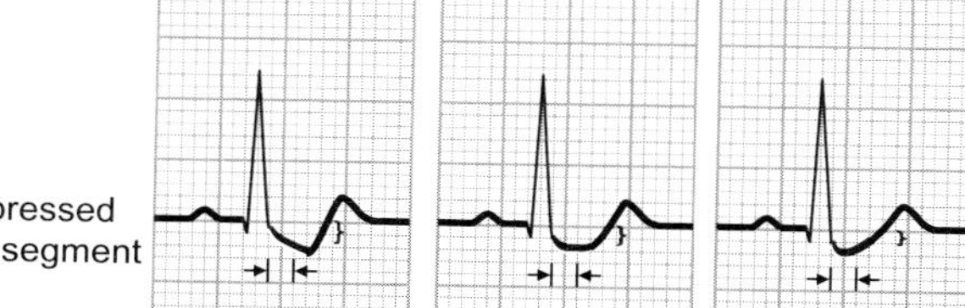

PR Segment

Significance: Represents the **time from the end of atrial depolarization to the onset of ventricular depolarization** during which the electrical impulse progresses from the AV node through the bundle of His, bundle branches, and Purkinje network to the ventricular myocardium.

ECG Characteristics

Onset and End: Begins with the end of the P wave and ends with the onset of the QRS complex.

Duration: Normally varies from about 0.02 to 0.10 second, but may be greater than 0.10 second if there is a delay in the progression of the electrical impulse through the AV node, bundle of His, or, rarely, the bundle branches.

Amplitude: Normally, flat (isoelectric).

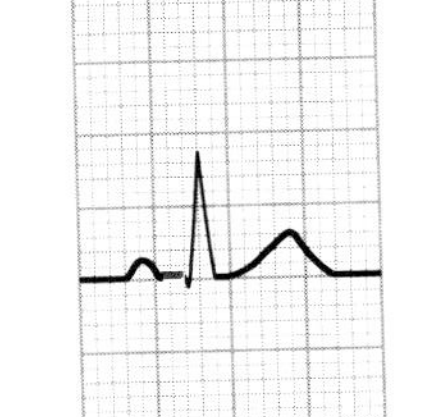

— = PR segment

TP Segment

Significance: Represents the **time from the end of ventricular repolarization to the onset of atrial depolarization** interval, the **space between two successive P-QRS-T complexes,** during which electrical activity of the heart is absent.

ECG Characteristics

Onset and End: Begins with the end of the T wave and ends with the onset of the following P wave.

Duration: 0.0 to 0.40 second or greater depending on the heart rate, being shorter when the heart rate is fast and longer when the heart rate is slow. (Example: heart rate about 120 or greater, TP segment 0 second; heart rate about 60 or less, TP segment 0.04 second or greater).

Amplitude: Usually flat (isoelectric).

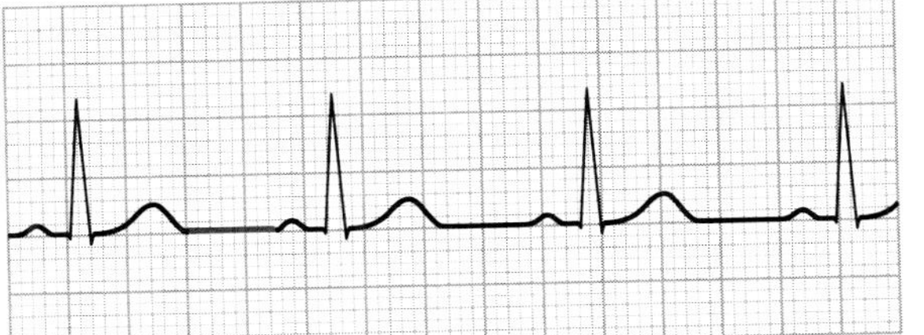

— = TP segment

Normal ECG Components

P Waves: Normally, each followed by a QRS complex.

Direction: Positive (upright) in leads I, II, aVF, and V_4-V_6. Negative (inverted) in lead aVR. Positive, negative, or diphasic in leads III, aVL, and V_1-V_3.

Duration: 0.10 second or less.

Amplitude: 0.5 to 2.5 mm.

Shape: Smooth and rounded.

QRS Complexes: 0.10 sec or less with generally narrow and sharply pointed waves.

Q waves: 0.04 second or less in duration and less than 25% of the height of the succeeding R wave.

Ventricular activation time (VAT): 0.05 second or less.

T Waves: Less than 5 mm in the standard limb and unipolar leads; less than 10 mm in the precordial leads.

PR Intervals: 0.10-0.20 sec.

QT Intervals: Less than half the preceeding R-R interval.

ST Segments: Flat, but may be elevated or depressed by no more than 1.0 mm, 0.08 second (2 small squares) after the J point.

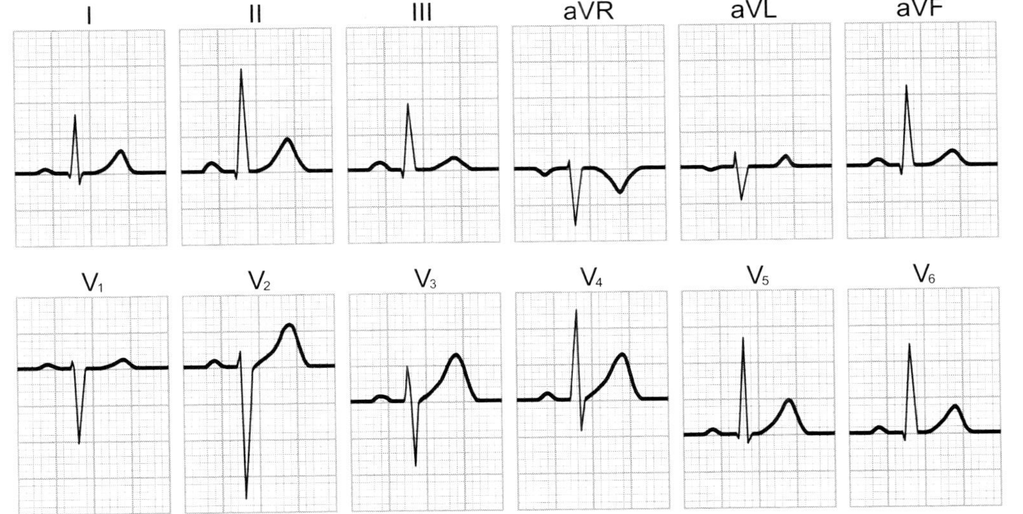

normal electrocardiogram

ECG Interpretation

The following is an outline of the steps in interpreting an ECG to determine the presence of an **arrhythmia** and its identity. The ECG interpretation may be performed in the order shown or in accordance with local prehospital or hospital protocols.

Arrhythmia Determination

A. Step One: Identify and analyze the QRS complexes.

1. Identify the QRS complexes.
2. Note the duration and shape of the QRS complexes.
3. Assess the equality of the QRS complexes.

B. Step Two: Determine the heart rate.

C. Step Three: Determine the ventricular rhythm.

D. Step Four: Identify and analyze the P, P´, F, or f waves.

1. Identify the P, P´, F, or f waves.
2. Determine the atrial rate and rhythm.
3. Note the relationship of the P, P´, F, or f waves to the QRS complexes.

E. Step Five: Determine the PR or RP´ Intervals and AV Conduction ratio.

1. Determine the PR (or RP´) intervals.
2. Assess the equality of the PR (or RP´) intervals.
3. Determine the AV conduction ratio.

F. Step Six: Determine the site of origin of the arrhythmia.

G. Step Seven: Identify the arrhythmia.

H. Step Eight: Evaluate the significance of the arrhythmia.

The following is an outline of the steps in interpreting a 12-lead ECG to determine the presence of an **acute myocardial infarction (AMI)** and its **location** and the estimated time of **onset.** The ECG interpretation may be performed in the order shown or in accordance with local prehospital or hospital protocols.

Acute Myocardial Infarction Determination

A. Step One: Identify any abnormally elevated or depressed ST segments and the leads where noted.

B. Step Two: Identify any abnormally tall or inverted T waves and the leads where noted.

C. Step Three: Identify any Q waves and the leads where noted.

D. Step Four: Identify any abnormally tall, deminished, or absent R waves and the leads where noted.

E. Step Five: Based on the above analysis, determine:

1. The presence or absence of an AMI.
2. The location of the AMI.
3. The estimated onset of the AMI.

Index

A

B

C

D

E

F

H

M

N

P

Q

R

S

T